MEMORY SICKNESS
AND OTHER STORIES

Phong Nguyen

Author Photo: Sarah Nguyen

Cover Photo: Hau Le

Book Design: Joel A. Bass

ISBN: 978-1-932418-41-5

Elixir Press
PO Box 27029
Denver, Colorado 80227

www.ElixirPress.com

Library of Congress Cataloging-in-Publication Data

Nguyen, Phong, 1978-
Memory Sickness, and Other Stories / Phong Nguyen.
p. cm.
ISBN 978-1-932418-41-5 (alk. paper)
I. Title.
PS3614.G95M46 2011
813'.6--dc22

2011000733

Elixir Press is a nonprofit literary organization.

MEMORY SICKNESS
AND OTHER STORIES

Phong Nguyen

Elixir Press

Contents

Acknowledgements

First and foremost I must thank my family, all of whom have made sacrifices so that I could have the time and comfort to write. This book and all books I dedicate to you.

There are numerous individuals and organizations whose support (both moral and financial) has been absolutely essential during the writing of this book: Debra and David Hellman; Jim and Dorothy Hershman; Crystal Keiley, for her extraordinary humanity; the UW-Milwaukee English Department, especially George Makana Clark, Kimberly Blaeser, and Mary Louise Buley Meissner; the AOP Fellowship; the staff of *cream city review* past and present, including but not limited to Erica Weiss, Stephen McCabe, Bayard Godsave, Christi Clancy, Suzanne Heagy, and Deb Brenegan; fiction friends Trudy Lewis, Eric Williamson, Don Lee, Matthew Salesses, Ben Percy, Amina Gautier; all of my colleagues and friends in the University of Central Missouri English Department, as well as our Dean, Gersham Nelson; my fellow *Pleiades* editors, Wayne Miller, Matthew Eck, Kevin Prufer, and Rose Marie Kinder. All of you, I deeply thank.

I would especially like to acknowledge the editors and readers who believed in these stories before anyone else did: Sven Birkerts, Bill Pierce, William Giraldi, and Jessica Keener of Agni (who published the title story "Memory Sickness," my first to appear in print); Amy Hempel, who judged the contest which led to publication in *Inkwell Journal* (as well as Alex Lindquist and Tina Tocco, who accepted "The Opposite of Gray"); David Lenson and all the editors at *Massachusetts Review*, where "Man Bites Dog" first appeared; Jeanne Leiby and *The Florida Review*, for first publishing "Made in Taiwan"; Ryan Call and Kelly Ford at *Phoebe*, for selecting "The Good China" for publication; Ron Mitchell, for his enthusiasm for "Body Art" and "The Death of an Ironist," both of which made their first appearance in *Southern Indiana Review*; Jeff Brewer, for publishing "Four Hundred and One" in *Portland Review*; Martin

Tucker at *Confrontation*, where "Manhattan Project" first appeared; Anna Shearer and the folks at *Meridian*, which first featured "220 Nickels"; W. A. Reed and Vicki Reed at the sadly now-defunct Wisconsin journal *Porcupine*, which published "The Ballad of John Gray" in its final issue.

Lastly, thank you to Dana Curtis, editor of Elixir Press, for giving all the stories in *Memory Sickness* a second life.

For Hien and Emily, who made me;

for Sarah, who made me again;

for Toby, Henry, and Benjy, who made me again.

MEMORY SICKNESS

Roth Chay

I'm sitting in a classroom of boys, our forearms laid out on the L-shaped desks, pale-sides up. My fingers are tucked into the palm and tensed, and my sleeve is pulled up to the elbow, as if waiting for a shot of adrenaline. This is what Teacher says, holding out his clenched hand in the same way: "Your heart is the size of your fist."

The girls are sitting in neat rows in the next room, learning the functions of their bodies from an overhead projector. I can hear the whir of the fan and the drone of the tape player through the thin divider. For the boys, the teacher decided on a more interactive approach. Their idea is that we are active learners and need the feel of three-dimensional space in order to believe what we see. "This is what your insides look like," Teacher says, opening up the front of a plastic model of the human anatomy.

"Yum," Chuck Wonicki says, sitting next to me, and a few kids chuckle. He's got spiky blonde hair and wears cologne. He keeps his backpack on the desk the whole class period, like he's ready to take off at any second.

~

I was eleven when I witnessed my first execution. Around dawn, I returned from combat, shaking in my joints, numb in the face. I could not unflex my fingers. The Vietnamese troops had repelled the Khmer army under steady fire, taking almost half our number, and when the barrage broke, the anticipation of death was even more acute in the silent, deep night. There in Chau Doc, no one could tell us why a man was now kneeling on the dirt, his hair riot with blood, picked at by flies. No one said why they carved out his insides, emptying onto the ground like spilled soup. It was a lesson in something, but no one knew what.

~

1

The organs in front of me now, carefully manufactured and glossed, look nothing like the outpour of blood and viscera that flowed from inside that man. They look clean and colorful and discrete, as though the human body were made to be labeled.

"If your intestines were to be stretched out, so that all its surface area were exposed, it would reach around the world," says Teacher, holding up a diagram of the digestive system showing the ridges of villi and microvilli tucked into the intestinal walls. "You could climb all the way down to China on your own intestines." He laughs. Some of the kids look nervously back at the four of us.

"What you lookin' at, fool?" my friend, Sen, says. He wears a sun visor, and he sports a skull earring that he bought at the flea market. "I ain't from China."

Before being taken to the camps, I lived in a village near the Thai border where fighting had been rare. My father was a music teacher who'd retreated into village life after our mother was committed, and he could no longer stand to see his kids playing in the streets with the children of gangsters. He could not have predicted that the new gangsters would be from villages like ours—that we would be the new gangsters.

He spent evenings patiently teaching me, his eldest son, to play the *tro*—a two-string fiddle that he could coerce to sound like flutes, like drums, like voices. "Once you learn the *tro*," he told me, "your ears are attuned to melody, and even birds and dogs sound like music."

My sisters were all singers, but only Teva learned to play the *tro* with me. Chann started on the *khim*, but he was young, and wouldn't remember anyway. There were also foreign instruments, from my father's travels in Europe. Ten different styles of violin, fifty books of music, along with seven children, filled his house—a retreat from the school and the daily trials of propaganda.

In 1975, the beginning of history on the revolutionary calendar, the Red Khmer decided to quicken the deaths of foreign-speaking scholars. They burned all of our books and instruments along with my father's body, freshly dead. Years later, in America, when I saw a man destroy his own electric guitar on TV, I became sick with anger.

~

Speaking in Cambodian, Arn points out that the skeleton in the corner of the Health classroom is that of a white man. Sen says that a white man would be ashamed to appear dead without pearly-white teeth. I point out that the whole bone structure has been bleached, because a white skeleton is more attractive than a brown-and-yellow one.

We talk in rounds, listening for the moment in the rhythm of conversation where our part belongs. When I first came here, the customs official gave a speech about local etiquette that the correspondent translated as best as she could; since then, I've often heard people on TV, or at school, go on in this way for great lengths of time. Perhaps this is why they say we are quiet people—we are waiting for our turn to speak.

~

On the straw-brown earth we paced the wire perimeter. We smoked cigarettes, but we could not talk. We were spoken to, not by people, but by loudspeakers. Before fighting for the revolution, we were made to understand the doctrines of the new society. Men and women are instruments of the state. Free agency is a counter-revolutionary idea bred from generations of imperialism. All titles and honorifics are forbidden—even terms of endearment, which show favoritism to one's family—and everyone henceforward will be referred to as a *mit*, a comrade.

If your sister survives into the new regime, a friend told me, and you see her again after the camps, you are expected to call her mit. None of my sisters lived through the purges, so I could never verify whether what he said was true or not.

~

Teacher says that by laughing during Anatomy class, we're

3

showing discomfort with our bodies. And we're showing disrespect for his classroom. But the words sound funny to us—like the names of alien civilizations: Medulla Oblongata; Angular Gyrus; Fallopian tubes. What they all refer to, far as I can tell, is as mysterious as the names they've been given.

Teacher's sense of humor is like this: "And I know you guys will like this one—" pointing to the inside of his arm, he says, "the Humerus! Our funny bone." We know bones. That much is familiar.

Outside our window, the track team runs in circles.

~

In the camps, there was a name for what afflicted us: "memory sickness." We were haunted by residual thoughts of comfort and family. Decadence distracted us from the purity of revolution. Particularly bad cases of memory sickness were considered untreatable. The infection could only be stopped by the death of its host. This is a lesson that we brought to America. Comfort kills.

But the cured were given guns, and the privilege of using them on the enemies of Khmer. I lay among them every night, hearing strains of melody in the still-afflicted regions of my brain. Bombs making music over our heads.

~

By the time Teacher is rolling a condom over the tip of a banana, the class has separated into fifteen different conversations, all of which are, at least, on the subject of human anatomy. As the steady hum of the film projector continues next door, I can sense his strength wearing down. It is a look that is familiar to me, where the eyes seem to wear their lids like hats and the chin barely holds in the jaw. The shoulders yield more to gravity. The arms lose their animation.

In the din of thirty loud voices cracking with hormones, he moves past us to the back of the room and flips on the film projector. Clicks the lights off. The screen shows a doctor calmly explaining the mechanics of breath. Over the most basic part of our brain we exert no conscious control. Hearts beat, and lungs aspirate, without our volition. In this way, he says, we are exactly like machines.

4

During the war, my father said: "America takes over your land and says that you are free. Cambodia gives weapons to half of its people and says that everyone is equal."

In the camp an older boy slipped up while repeating the party dictum, accidentally using the older French slogan, "egalité." He was shot through the eye. I think of this when I hear the word equality, no matter how much I remind myself what it is supposed to mean. I was eleven, and the only thing I knew was that, if there were two equalities, my equality would be the one holding the gun.

Chuck Wonicki turns toward me in the half-dark and says, "Dude, you stink."

I look back at him, reading the mock disgust on his face. He's a kid trying out toughness, to see how it feels to control another person. I almost want to warn him. How consuming such power can be.

Instead, I point at the filmstrip like I'm too wrapped up in the respiratory system to give a shit what he says.

"Why don't you smack that bitch?" Sen says to me. "He just said you stink, man. He's talkin' like he know you."

"I know." I say with a shrug.

"Man, if you don't smack him, I'll fuckin' do it." Sen stands up, in middle of the film strip. Part of his shoulder and collar are visible as shadows on the screen.

Our anatomy instructor, Mr. Merrick, a gym teacher, though three times Sen's size, acts as if he isn't there. He's an ex-hippie, a health nut, who coaches the rock climbing team. But he must know his share of vets too—men for whom killing is a rote process, like arithmetic. A simple matter of subtraction.

Sen shouts at Chuck in street Cambodian, "Play dead, bitch. If you talk, I'll beat you till you can't move, because dead men shouldn't be talking. But if you sit there like a good corpse, I'll leave you alone, 'cause you're just another fuckin' body."

5

In the harshness of that minute, while the film runs on about respiration, everyone is bilingual, understanding Sen's words as though it were meant for the whole class, which passes the moment silently, and begins to understand our silence too.

Realizing that some gesture is needed, some new focus for the class, I pull out a Lucky Strike and ignite the end, sucking in the harsh unfiltered air. The light between the projector and the screen is suddenly cloudy and visible.

"Roth," Mr. Merrick says to me in his most temperate, teacherly voice, "go and see Vice Principal Edwards, right now. And put that cigarette out. This is Health class, dammit."

~

For weeks we made tracks across the country, patrolling the border, installing local overseers from the Red army. On every stop, I wanted to be one of those left behind, but each time I was herded in with the other soldiers instead. We were kids from the country, every one of us, and all we knew how to do was tend crop and tame animals. I knew how to handle a *tro* better than I could fire an assault rifle. As a unit, we seemed to be chasing death, and it is only through accident that it eluded our capture for so long.

When we reached Chau Doc we fortified ourselves and prepared for a skirmish with the Vietnamese. We soon found the town already emptied, having been used as a military post, and then as a supply station, and then vacated. We settled there, because we were told to do so, but now that we were anchored I began to feel that maybe chasing death was not quite so bad as spending the nights waiting for it.

If our troop had not killed a Vietnamese for days, commander Meng would find someone near him to blame. Even the red army was not immune. Calling us all together, he would shout, "Who are the useless ones among you? Who is holding back the revolution? Who is weak and fearful? Who can I kill without regret?"

~

In Providence, I learned the virtue of standing out. More than happiness even, it seemed, everyone desired to stand out. Boys wore patches and brand names. Girls wore glitter and big earrings. For sports, everyone wanted to be exceptional, and heroic—the first to be chosen for the team. In my home country, you would never want to be picked out of a line.

Nowadays, I don't have a choice. In a strange way I have succeeded at what people here strive for, without any effort on my part. "The pathology of America," my History teacher says, "is to simultaneously yearn to be different and despise those who are different."

In the Vice Principal's office, I unsling my backpack and fall into a chair. I scan the room for a magazine or pamphlet, like they might have at the nurse's office. Not even a poster. Out of boredom, I dig out my book from English and start in on the homework—a book called *Lord of the Flies*. It's all about kids stranded on an island, who have to survive on their own until the adults come to save them. In the meantime, they revert to a tribal state and all of it turns to hell. It's a pretty quick read, and a lot better than most of the other stuff they're pushing. But as I'm reading I keep wondering what happens after it ends. Like, what do they do after they're saved from the island? What happens when the wild ones return home to their English manors?

What finally led me to flee was the construction of a wall. Before, when the perimeter had been invisible, it seemed impossible to escape. Now that I could see the barriers, they looked not nearly as formidable as I'd thought. But for a long time I could only cast longing looks at it, as though the mere flirtation would consummate the escape. At first, I had no thought of doing it alone, so I had to broach the subject with other soldiers in subtle and shadowy ways.

Then, during the monsoon season, I approached one boy a little older than me who had a gentle, girl's face and a war-weary voice. "The rain looks like it'll last a while, comrade. You want to seek shelter?" I asked him, although we were already covered from the rain in our enclosure. He responded with a look that was naked

7

of feeling, either solicitous or treacherous. Then he glanced at the command post the way I'd been glancing at the wall, longingly. Just a movement of the eyes, but it was telling. By turning me in, he would have been rewarded, and I would have been killed. There are two equalities.

If the missionaries were right and there is such a thing as hell, I know that I could survive there. You must store up all your evils to repent for later, when you are not beset by so much killing, and fear of killing. For now you must stay alive long enough to know such leisure. Some sinners confess on their deathbeds. Some sinners confess on Sundays. But most of us live with chronic pangs of conscience like migraines. All I know is that no one is guiltless. We make mistakes.

Vice Principal Edwards busts in with my Lucky Strikes in a plastic baggie, like evidence. We're a big school and I suppose I should be flattered that he showed up himself. I know it's an act, but I never fully cast off the fear of authority.

"Hey kid, you know what you did?" He looks even more serious than when he's speaking in the auditorium. His face is as red as his hair.

I nod.

"Kid?" He says. His usual routine is to call you Mr. So-and-so, so I think maybe he can't handle the pronunciation.

After a silence, I manage to let out a "What?"

"Do you know what you did?" He asks. And as we enter another drawn-out silence, I almost want to break apart—to unburden to him, not just my rebel moment in the middle of third period, but the whole confluence of moments before it: the heaviness of the guns in our hands; the rice we seized from our comrades, the farmers; the awkward smiles we wore during executions, to prove that we were immune to indulgences of sympathy.

"I lit a cigarette." I finally answered.

"You broke the law." He said. "You're not in Danang now, kid. You can't just do any fool thing you want."

"Who's from Danang?" I said.

"Don't try to patronize me, son," he says, sliding the Lucky Strikes across the table. Then he says something sharp in Vietnamese, which sends an electric coil down my back and settles in the groin where, no matter what Anatomy says, a soldier feels his most mortal fears. A host of unwilling memories comes upon me, and I start to go faint. My vision blackens at the edges. But I remain strangely conscious.

Principal Edwards doesn't miss a beat before pronouncing his sentence: the mandatory two weeks' suspension. "Smoke on that," he says, like it's a one-liner in a movie, and this is his moment. I notice he's left the pack of cigs on the table, as if daring me to take another one.

After he leaves the room, I right myself on the chair and go back to my reading. He might haunt me, but when he looks at me, I know that he is haunted too. The thought of it makes me less lonely.

I don't ever talk about what happened after the monsoon, because the things I remember are not the things that people talk about. If they ask, I'll tell them about "triumph over adversity" instead. If they probe, I'll say how I "struggled nobly" for "freedom," against all the odds. What I will not do is talk about the long walk to America, because that is where children lay dead on the side of the road, and you are happy not to be one of them. And because someday I may have to escape again, and I do not want you to know how I can be caught.

MAN BITES DOG

L.B. Gray

L.B.'s new mother lived at 971 Hope Street on the East Side of Providence. He had written it down on a slip of paper in his pocket, in case he forgot. But for the first time in months, he found it practical to remember his home address, and even his telephone number. Without thinking about it, he started to memorize other details: the date of his arrival; his sixth grade class schedule; Ms. Gray's license plate number; her cell phone; email. She was beginning to imprint herself on his memory, the way he had never let the others do.

So when Ms. Gray saw L.B. actually open the refrigerator, take out some bread, cheese, deli meat, and condiments to make himself a sandwich, she joked, "Don't get too comfortable—you never know when I'm gonna get tired of you." For some reason, the ease of her threat made him feel even more settled there.

Anila Gray didn't carry herself like other moms: her figure was bony and sharp; her expressions were puppy-like and exaggerated; her sweater was always two sizes too large in the winter, as though she wished someone bigger than her could fill it; and in the summer, she wore a paint-splattered noodle-strap blouse that didn't fully cover her midriff, with fringy cut-off jeans.

She didn't carry herself like other moms, and in fact Ms. Gray was a single girl who spent half the year taking care of stray cats, lost dogs, and other kids just like L.B., and the other half working as a travelling nurse. L.B. thought she didn't act much like a nurse either.

"Hey," she called out to L.B., snapping her fingers in front of his face. From anyone else, this would have been rude, but coming from her, it was only further evidence of their familiarity. To him, it meant that she saw him as imaginative, almost other-worldly. "Spaced out," is the word she used over the phone. "Hello-o? Don't you have school?"

L.B. popped to attention, after a delay sufficient enough to establish his remoteness from the world. "I think I should stay home again," he said, "I mean, all we're doing today is this assembly

11

meeting, and I could just sit around and study all day instead."

Ms. Gray laughed in a way that looked like she'd lose her cereal. "The weird thing about you is you're serious," she said. "You *would* sit around and study all day."

She shook her head, laughed again. L.B. waited.

"Sorry," she said, "I have to go over to Paul's house and watch TV today, and I can't have you here in the house by yourself. You'll just have to live through another day of school."

"Duh, we have TV. Why doesn't Paul come over here, and I'll stay in my room?" L.B. suggested.

"I thought you didn't like Paul," she said, with half a smile on her face.

"No, he doesn't like me," he replied with a pleading look. She wasn't like the other moms in this way either: he could always persuade her with an argument. With Ms. Gray, there was never a *because I said so.*

L.B. was a big kid with loose brown hair and cheeks that looked like they'd just been slapped. He wore shirts with collars, pants with pleats, and a belt with a horn-buckle. Paul complained that Ms. Gray's new son dressed like a Waldo. Ms. Gray thought his look was more ironic: a remark on 1950s reruns.

L.B. watched Paul pull up in his cream-colored Jetta, and grab a worn-out backpack from the passenger side, yanking the door open with a squeak, slamming it, and jogging up to the door. L.B. had never seen someone that age with a backpack, with the exception of Paul. The dogs barked at him from behind the garage door.

Paul walked in before L.B. had a chance to duck into his room. He was sitting on the sofa with his biology textbook.

"Hey, L.B.," Paul said, with a glossy smile, "Your mom said you were sick."

"Um...yeah," he said, not wanting to be inconsistent, but not wanting to commit to a lie either.

"You look about fit enough to go ten rounds with Tyson," Paul said. Kids like L.B. are always getting groomed for boxing or football by men like Paul, who look at children and see the potential for physical prowess.

L.B. mumbled incoherently. Paul didn't notice. He was listening to the sound of the shower running.

"That your mom in the bathroom?" he asked. L.B. nodded, and went back to his reading.

Paul stared hard. "Don't people talk in this house?"

"Yes," L.B. said, startling himself to attention. "Sorry. I was reading about photosynthesis and stuff."

Paul smiled. "Smart kid."

L.B. thought that, the way Paul said it, smart sounded like something you did not want to be. He suddenly wished that he had Ms. Gray all to himself today. She would revel in his distractedness.

"I'm gonna go to my room," L.B. announced. Closing the door behind him, L.B. sat against the window. The walls were blank except for spots of glue and tacky—remnants of the room's past occupants. In the garage, the dogs' aggressive snarls subsided into a whimper, and their paws scraped gently on the heavy aluminum door.

From his room, he heard the TV shriek to life on the other side of the wall. Talk show bedlam ensued. But over the volume, L.B. could still hear the creak of Ms. Gray's bed, and Paul's low moans of pleasure or triumph through the plaster.

She and Paul were three years in when Anila felt easy enough with their relationship to make demands. For longer than she cared to admit, Paul represented the kind of man that had always snubbed her in her youth: bold to the point of recklessness, charming to the point of deviousness, and irrepressibly sexual. Like a Kennedy, she thought. Though Anila could never cast herself as the trophy wife, sitting atop a float with the other bluebloods in a campaign season parade, her hand waving as on a turnstile. So she met his presence in her life with equal measures of wariness and gratitude, and alternately hoarded his company and spurned it.

She found that six months was the perfect length of time for this kind of indulgence, after which she would fly away to Nevada, to treat victims of brush fire, or to Florida, for hurricane relief. Most jobs were not so dramatic, but each one had, in a small way, its own nobility.

When she began to ask Paul, tentatively, to water her plants every

13

week and dust every month she was gone, he was relieved. He had no time to take on extra assignments, but Anila's hesitation to oblige him in anything had always seemed to suggest her lack of debt to him; while the thousands of hot meals and clean dishes and laundry loads that passed from her hands to his could have been so many silver dollars accumulating over the years into bagsful of change, whose weight he had now begun to feel.

They lay together in the bed watching *People's Court*, a show that neither of them cared for particularly. Paul grabbed a pack of cigarettes from the nightstand. As he lit one up and sat there leaning on the headboard, Anila was a little disappointed with him for being so cliché. "What time do you have to be back?" Anila asked, turning toward him slowly.

Paul looked out on the room through a haze. He looked more serious than usual, more human in his nakedness. "One," he said absently.

"Do you want lunch or something?" she asked, but he was in a thinking mood, and did not reply. Men, Anila noticed, stagger in their lives between depletion and renewal, like housecats. Now he was enervated, but if they stayed in bed together long enough, he would be invigorated soon and want to start up again. "I'll make you a sandwich," she said, hopping to her feet and out the door.

Paul worked in local news, and he raced cars on weekends. He was a town personality, and most people around Providence knew and liked him. He didn't know what it was with L.B. Foster kids always came a bit screwed up, he figured.

He blamed her neighbors for planting the seeds. They'd adopted kids from all over the place, and seemed to be growing their own little United Nations over there. They had a girl from Ghana, and one from China; they had boys from Romania, Cambodia, and Peru. Paul was a man who believed in charity, but taking strangers into your house to appease your sense of guilt made you a sucker in his book. There were better ways to give to the community that are harmonious with personal gain, which do not involve sacrificing ones own time or sanity.

Broadcasting was Paul's way of giving back. Whenever his team broke open a political scandal (which Rhode Island was full of), or exposed some so-called business for the fraud it perpetrated on the public, he felt a rush of adrenaline that he came to associate with civic pride. The two were coincident. So he never felt the need to drain himself with unnecessary burdens, as did Ms. Gray. Yet he always found himself having to deal with the consequences of her wide open heart, such as those stray dogs she kept, which she insisted he care for when she took off for three months to work as a travelling nurse. And then there were the kids.

This weekend Paul was charged with taking L.B. to the Red Sox game in Boston. He'd agreed to it because some months ago the thought of playing father—complete with matching baseball caps, cute conversation, and stadium philosophy—appealed to him. They hopped an afternoon train and spent an hour bumming around the shops near Fenway before the event. Now he and L.B. were sitting only a sprint away from the action on game day; the younger watching with quiet veneration, the older with patient restraint, broken only occasionally by the mania of the crowd when a line drive would leave the fate of the game in doubt, or an unexpected bunt would cause a mad rush for the ball, and Paul would let out an idle cheer, out of nothing more stirring than home-team feeling.

Instead of sports talk, Paul engaged L.B. in a Q&A about his new mom. What did he think of her? Did she go anywhere during the day? Does she get a lot of phone calls? Do other men ever come to the house?

Not wanting to be inaccurate, L.B. said that sometimes Ms. Gray did talk on the phone, and that he saw other people at the door sometimes, even if they never came inside. Sensing that the kid was getting uncomfortable, Paul quit asking questions, and seethed quietly until the game went into a tenth inning.

"She's gonna leave, you know," he said finally.

L.B. nodded his head as though he already knew. He wanted Paul to believe that Ms. Gray told him everything.

"Yup," he said, affecting a southern drawl, with a fake-funny curl in his lip, "She gonna fly the coop. Kick up the dust. Get the hell out of Dodge…It's gonna be just you and me here for a while. This whole baseball thing is a test. She wants to see if we can get along together…and we do, right?"

L.B. got the distinct feeling that Paul meant the opposite of what he was saying. A few years before, L.B. was at a school where they played the opposite game every Friday. One kid broke out crying when he asked to go to the bathroom, and the teacher kept saying "No, you may *not*." In opposite world, she was really saying "yes, go ahead," but he couldn't get over the word "no," so he just sat there until a dark spot began to form on the leg of his corduroys.

On Monday afternoon, in the middle of eighth period math, L.B. screamed. When Mrs. Jenkins went over to see what was wrong, he screamed again—a shrill, agonizing sound, nothing like an animal howl. The bell rang by the time they got him calmed down and out of the classroom, and Mrs. Jenkins sat down with Ms. Willis, the guidance counselor. Once they decided to get his mother involved, L.B. began to scream again, and wouldn't stop until Ms. Willis promised to talk with him alone.

In private session, Ms. Willis didn't learn much about L.B. except that, if she tried to contact Ms. Gray, he would get uneasy. She could see in his file that he was a new student, and a foster, and she suspected from his behavior that it was some kind of abuse—a situation potentially beyond the scope of her experience, and probably a case for state social workers. Luckily, Mrs. Jenkins had the presence of mind to call Ms. Gray anyway and get her to the school before L.B. knew about it. Anila walked into the room looking like a girl being sent to the principal's office, and gave L.B. a quick hug. She got the story three different times from three different people, then brought L.B. home.

Ms. Willis did manage to get a couple words out of him before he left though. She had asked him where he slept at night, and he said "I live at 971 Hope Street on the East Side of Providence."

On the way home, Anila shook her head, adjusting the driver's side window every now and then with nervous intensity. Then she started making digs at the teachers and administrators of Providence Public School. How could they make such a big stink about a kid letting off steam? Anila sure as hell felt like crying out at the end of a twelve-hour shift, and the more she thought about it, the more she admired L.B. for not giving a shit what other people might think about a boy who screams his head off in school.

Paul felt pathetic following his girlfriend around in the middle of the day. It introduced all kinds of uncomfortable questions about the direction his life was taking. In general, he preferred being in the field, making news, but Anila's recent distance from him, and her choice to take a six-month break to go work on an Indian reservation in South Dakota, was maddening. Then, when he was pulling up for a lunch visit and saw her drive away in the old Volkswagon, he had to know where she was going. Still, he felt like the bad guy on daytime soaps who followed women from a distance, rather than the guy who took her in his arms and owned her, the way he'd always thought of himself.

Anila only left after Paul promised he'd get the kid off to school in the mornings, and pick him up in the afternoon. Other than that, she said, he was pretty self-sufficient. He was the most independent kid she'd ever known, and as long as he had plenty to eat, and got outside every now and then, he could withstand a nuclear blast. "Like a cockroach," Paul said, earning him a scowl from under her hair.

Two hours earlier, she sat in the parking lot of the school, explaining to L.B. how much the Lakota tribes needed good nursing help, and what a good thing it would be for her to answer the call. She didn't want to send him back to the foster home, she said. He was too old now to keep shuttling from home to home, and if he only stuck around while she was doing her job, then he could be adopted officially. Paul would take good care of him in the meantime. She'd be home by the summer.

L.B. scoffed. "Pff...Paul," he said.

"Honey," she said, laying her hand protectively over his knee. "Honey," she repeated, "Paul is not the enemy."

L.B. could not stay focused on his book, *Of Mice and Men*. There was a character, Lennie, who was real big and strong, but simple-minded. All he wanted to do in the world was tend rabbits, but whenever he got a hold of one, he'd wind up killing it, or hurting it badly. At one point he breaks a woman's neck by accident, and the rest of the men try and hunt him down. With only a couple pages left, L.B. couldn't concentrate; eyes tired, ears distracted by dogs scratching on the door.

Outside, he saw Gian and Paco, his neighbors, switching pitches and at-bats. Whenever Paco made a hit—because he was the better player—he'd run at full speed, as if it were a true game, and after landing on a base he'd call out, "ghost man on first," or "ghost man on third." The sun was setting over the forest, shared by their backyards. After watching for almost an hour, L.B. began to see what they saw: a sandy field; a team of men, serious about play, standing at the ready, or cheering them on from the stands. Then, as the light waned, and it was no longer possible to track the ball as it flew at you, Gian and Paco took their bat, ball, and glove inside with them where, L.B. imagined, a full table awaited them.

The dogs had gone missing. Paul had heard them barking into the night, then they suddenly went quiet, but he was already halfway asleep and hadn't thought much of it. But in the morning, when he found the garage empty except for the bags of dog food and stacks of bottled water, he started cursing himself for his negligence. He hated to give Anila another reason not to trust him.

Paul went next door and pounded. Don, the serial adopter, answered in his robe. "What's the occasion, Paul?" Don asked.

"Our dogs are missing," he said.

"I'm sorry to hear it," Don replied. "Should I have the boys help you look for 'em?"

Paul gave a bitter smile—a smile that said, *you wish it were that easy.* "I think it was your boys that did it," he ventured, prodding the lapel of his robe with an accusatory finger.

"Excuse me?" Don said. "The kids were in bed long before your dogs were. We could hear them barking all night, practically."

"Well, apparently someone over here thought they'd have a little fun with my noisy dogs, eh?" Paul said. He had a residual feeling that a cameraman was filming the encounter from over his shoulder.

"I think you'd better calm down, and then come talk to me,

okay Paul? Now, if you'll excuse me, I have to get the kids ready for church." Don tried shutting the door, but Paul's experienced foot came between it and the doorjamb.

He put his best game face on. "Look. Don. I know you want to think the best of your kids and all, but you've got people here who come from places where dog is on the menu, am I wrong?"

"If you don't take your foot out of this door, Paul, I swear I'll call the police," Don said.

Paul knew where a confrontation ended. He used the P.A.L. system: Police, Assault, or Lawsuit. Anything short of being arrested, attacked, or sued, was just another fence to be hurdled.

From his bedroom window, L.B. watched Paul storm back toward the house, slamming the screen door. Winter had started to show on the eaves: frost edged inward on the tile, and the gutter drip froze in mid-leak. Outside, a light snow dusted everything, settling into the fallen leaves like milk in cups.

There was a rule of thumb that Paul used to determine whether a story went to press, or died in development: " 'Dog Bites Man' is not a story. 'Man Bites Dog' is a story." This simple equation helped him dodge all the marshmallow stories that other outlets were covering, and focus on the protein-rich items that put muscle into the daily news. That Monday he was covering an abuse story at the senior citizen's center, which involved several employees on the government dole. They'd shot the bit early in the morning, and finished cutting it, and were about to send the clip out to the network, when he got a call from the school. It seemed that a student had broken into the school last night and let loose three dogs in the guidance counselor's office.

A part of Paul wanted to punish L.B. for being so screwed up in the head that he would do that. The sick part of him was impressed that an eleven-year old could carry off such a project on his own; though he thought it would have worked better if it weren't his dogs. But the part that won out was denial.

"Why are you calling me to tell me you picked up a few stray dogs?" Paul said.

"I think you know, Mr. Gray," the principal said.

"The name's Tibbets. There is no Mr. Gray," he said, "and no I don't know why you're calling me at work to tell me this."

"Can you guess?"

A silence ensued. Telephone silence.

"I dunno. You're lonely?" he said.

Anila came home early when she learned she was pregnant, a couple of weeks after L.B. freed their dogs and quit the school. The administration agreed not to inform the police—which would have put a blot on his record for the rest of his juvenile years—as long as he did not continue to attend PPS. The first thing Anila said when she got home was, "Looks like you get to stay home and study all the time now, huh L.B.?" He smiled and shrugged. Paul's expression was flat as a skipping stone.

At home in bed, Paul and Anila celebrated the coming of the baby with Chinese food delivery. She hadn't begun to feel the full-on cravings yet, but Anila wanted to establish the pattern of unorthodox eating—it was one of the strange charms of burgeoning life. They talked as they ate, about Anila's time in South Dakota, about Paul's last assignment, about the baby-to-be, and about L.B. When Anila thought she sensed Paul hinting at sending him back to foster care, she dropped her chopsticks into the mu-shu delivery box.

"You can't be serious, Paul," she said. "Just because he mucks up a little bit now and then? From what you tell me, you weren't always mister do-right in your adolescence."

"He's eleven," Paul emphasized, "eleven. If a kid tortures cute little animals at eleven years old, what do you think he's gonna be up to at seventeen?"

"You don't know that he tortured them, Paul; you're exaggerating. Besides, here's a kid who has been without real parental guidance for most of his life. If you want him to do something dangerous, send him back to foster care." They shared a pained silence.

"I'm not talking about foster care," Paul said, "I'm talking about Don and Rebecca next door. Those guys will take in anybody, and they haven't heard about the dogs yet...At least, they don't know L.B. is responsible."

Anila had been ready to leap at any foolish suggestion and

deflect it with her practiced indignity and overweening sense of righteousness. But she paused, surprised at how appealing the idea seemed at first—to have L.B. live so near by, a friend and neighbor, without having to be his constant ward and master.

"It's a tough choice to make, I know," Paul said, putting his hand on the slight curve of her belly, "but…"

At that, he let the nobility of her imagined sacrifice insinuate itself.

The thin walls leaked only this much intelligence into L.B.'s bedroom: that he could be sent back. It did not matter whether or not a decision had been made; if the topic were open, it was only a matter of time. He felt no particular remorse upon having this revelation, only a calm resolve to do what needed to be done. And as soon as he felt it, his body submitted to sleep.

The next morning, a Tuesday, L.B. left the house in his usual button-down and pleated pants, his pocket stuffed with a wad of cash from Ms. Gray's top drawer. He walked down College Hill to the canal, then crossed the bridge downtown, passing the public library on his way to Power street. At the corner of Washington, there was a streetlight, a newspaper dispenser, a post office mailbox, and a two-headed parking meter, all bolted to the sidewalk. Across the street was a gun store called, simply, "Guns N' Ammo," and next to it, a tattoo parlor with a busy front-window display with a neon sign reading "Voodoo Tattoo."

In his fantasy, he saw himself walking into the gun store, putting all the cash down on the counter, and walking away with a hand-sized pistol. Of course he knew that fantasy was no good, so as an alternative he imagined walking in as soon as the clerk was away from the front register, and running behind the counter to grab one of the display pieces, and hopping the desk to make his escape. But every scenario he imagined had consequences that he couldn't quite stomach. Inwardly, he abused himself for having the ability to see the eventual outcome of things. If only he could act, without anticipation, without consideration, he would make things right again for him and Ms. Gray.

The streetlight winked its red eye, and the walking-man symbol appeared below it. L.B. shuffled slowly across the street, his shoes feeling suddenly tight in their laces. When he reached the curb, he had the inexplicable feeling of having undergone some severe trial, like flood, or famine. He stood there while the traffic light turned from green to yellow to red to green again, then walked through the jangling door of the tattoo parlor.

The Opposite of Gray

Chuck Wonicki

Waste Management, India Point
1996

The sky burns pink like raw meat. Low tide smell washes over the city on a low-grazing cloud. At 5 a.m., the sun and the moon hang together, and it's so early I can barely tell the difference.

Mounting the trash truck with one hand leaves the other free to plug up my nose. A rookie habit. But already the route is a kind of ritual—the shrimpers passing under East Providence bridge; the joggers; the hangovers; the retarded kid on the corner waiting too early for the bus, clutching a pinwheel; the guy who watches us through the window every Sunday, thinking "The trash truck driver is a spy."

Today, for some reason, instead of hiding behind a curtain, he's out on the lawn, walking the perimeter of his property. A human fence. He watches us empty his two aluminum bins—stares at us really—and blinks, like we're figments in a dream that he wants to erase.

Warwick Penitentiary, A-Block
1987

The only bright thing in this prison is Television. *Wheel of Fortune. Donahue.* Soaps. I never had time for it when I was a kid: I got out of school for the day, my folks wanted me to stay away from the house. Far back as I can remember, I've had to break into my own bedroom to sleep, much less fill the days with professional wrestling and music television. I never owned a door-key. And when I finally ran away for good, I took the damn TV with me.

In here, they screen all the programs. But everything is screened. It's the only way to be completely safe, they say. If you relax the code, then the ordinary, everyday feuds become killing affairs. But

23

I don't see that happening, to be honest. The only screaming I hear comes from the bathroom. It's like all we eat is peanut butter, raisins, lunchmeat and soda. Food is engineered for anal discomfort. It moves through our pipes faster than Zep. Keeps us up at night. Takes the fight out. Not that there's any fight at all among us.

What a sorry bunch of inmates. As a kid, I had a vision of prison life: The quiet guy with the Manson beard. The black bunkmate with a soulful voice and a sob story. The innocent guy; the brute; the bitch. Spanish mafia. I'm not saying we're all white collar types. We're not. But it ain't Alcatraz either. The best company I've got is a guard who tells me stupid things about his life outside. Like waiting in line at the DMV and they close for the day just as his number is called up.

Providence Public High School, Truant
1983

Fifteen years old I get my first pair of shades, red as the devil. From the Stopmart. They go with the canvas shoes, gel-spiked hair, and suntan. Torn denim. Ear pierced. But I've worn the lenses too long and next day all I can see with my naked eyes is a green wash, like the whole city is photosynthesizing.

On the color wheel they have up on the wall in the art room, the opposite of red is green, and if I'd 'a bought those Wizard-of-Oz, emerald-city glasses instead, afterwards the world would have ran red, like the first plague.

Stop or go? My streetlight flashes green.

Waste Management, India Point
1996

Home from work after picking up Carla's kid, Anthony, I empty my pockets into the hand basket in the kitchen. I still can't get used to owning my own set of keys. The certainty of knowing that they will always fit in certain places. The fear of losing them.

Prison guards hold the keys. My parents hold the keys.

I guess you can always blame the parents. But taking care of

Tony, now, after ten years in the pen for manslaughter, I have a real appreciation for forgiveness. And, though my own folks never visited me the whole ten years, I don't hold a grudge. But I don't visit them either.

Tony, nine years old, wants to know what "man's laughter" is. I bet he read one of Carla's letters. Or mis-read it, anyway. What else did he find in there?

You can't always be right up front with a kid. "What do you think it is, *señor?*" He's taking Spanish in school, and the only way I know of to help out is to drop words here and there.

"Um..." He has a lip-biting stare that says he's trying to avoid getting into trouble. "Like, tickling?"

I nod slowly. Then I fire off the tickles. He wriggles like a pig. Anthony watches pro wrestling every day, but when the fingers are flying all he does is tuck in his limbs and squirm.

WARWICK PENITENTIARY, A-BLOCK
1994

I finish high school in the pen. I figure I spend more time doing Math and English in here, just counting the days and writing letters to my lawyer. I'm hammering out one right now on an old Remington (six sentences in, and I've already used several phrases that sound like bad legal thrillers: "just cause," "double jeopardy," "due process"). We don't use computers in here, and they don't allow pens or pencils, or even feathers dipped in ink. Technologically speaking, we're stuck at about 1940, toward the end of the depression.

One guy in here started a newsletter, "Prose and Cons," and he got every literate dick on A-block to pitch in a piece. Mine started out being about understaffing in the warden's office, but then the ranks got hold of it and it turned out to be about the prison work ethic. Funny how you think you've said one thing, and it turns out that isn't what you said at all. My mistake. That's why it's called the corrections facility.

I make some quick calculations. If I spend eight hundred more days in here, then that could be divided up into twenty thousand hours, which is a million minutes, or sixty million seconds. A stoptimer like they use in the Olympics can accurately measure time in thousandths of seconds, of which I have sixty billion remaining to my term. To go on with partial numbers, fractions of fractions, yields a number that forever approaches, but never becomes, infinity. Everything is bounded by numbers. Comforting, I think.

PROVIDENCE PUBLIC HIGH SCHOOL, TRUANT 1986

I'm at the arcade with two of my buddies and one fatty who tagged along. The screens all emit a soft blue radiance into the room, like perpetual twilight. Each of us is tapping on consoles, maneuvering joysticks, watching ninjas get hacked up by some Rambo with pointed pecs.

"Hey, why do you think dudes have nipples?" I ask Jimbo.

"I dunno, Chuck," he answers. Jimbo is a joke. He's the one you expect to see picking up your garbage some day, or pacing around a prison cell. Not me. I play it safe, even when taking risks. "Why do you think Will has tits?" We crack up.

Will, the fatty, starts talking to me. It's like he doesn't even hear Jimbo:

"You know, male mammals have nipples 'cause they actually have mammary glands. They can produce milk, just like mothers do. Yeah, if the females are all dead or missing or something, then the men can actually breast-feed the babies. Freaky, huh?" Jimbo and Dan are smirking, and I've got the serious game face on, the ninja-slaughter face. Even my pinky is seeing action now.

"That's some sick shit, Will," I say.

"Speaking of titties," says Dan. "Angel knows you bagged Carla."

I freeze up, and just a second of distraction causes my Rambo to lose his life. He's getting pounded by a big boss, the ninja leader. Continue? Insert two quarters. "No fuckin' way. How the hell, man? Did you tell him?"

"No, man." Dan looks like he's enjoying himself. He can't stop smiling. He gets off on that shit. The instigator. "He knew you were sweatin' his girl. And now she's pregnant."

26

Tony is on the phone and the TV. The video game he's playing is cutesy, but action-packed. Something Japanese. His phone buddy is Japanese too, I think. A techno whiz kid. Future engineer.

"C'mon, we're gonna visit Mama," I say. Kid stays where he's sitting on the carpet. Just the mention of his mother and lockjaw sets in. "Get in the car, or the snake goes back to the pet store." He shuffles around to get ready. I don't care what the childcare professionals say: bargaining works.

We're hit with one of those middle-of-the-day storms, where night and day alternate. Wipers on, wipers off. The sky is black in some places, completely white in others. Checkerboard. I let Tony take his Gamestation along, and he's making little crosses with his thumbs, oblivious to all the signs from above.

They've got his mama in an observation room, for visitation. A horde of doctors stands around in the hallway, muttering conspiratorially. I can sniff out the interns. They haven't decided yet whether the rest of us are human beings, or just subjects.

Inside, she's sitting at the end of a long table, as if expecting guests for dinner. She's wearing hospital blues, and her usually oily hair is sculpted into stalagmites. She's got wristbands on—that was the fashion when we were kids—which she uses to cover up the scar tissue. Now every time I see aerobics on TV, I will imagine those same deep red lines underneath all of their fuzzy armlets.

"Baby, how are you?" She asks, turning mommy so quick I almost forget who she is, how she got here. She pockets the pack of Lucky Strikes she'd been handling.

Tony says nothing at first, and I'm about to nudge him with an elbow when he comes out with, "You're the one in the loony. How're you doing?"

Carla laughs, nervous. She's not yet used to her new, sardonic son. "Did you write a thank-you card to the Fagley's?"

I cut in. "It's on our to-do list." It's too much to explain to a committed woman that the family she left her kid with got divorced, soon after they took him on.

"When do you get out?" He asks. He's got Puerto Rican hair, like his mother.

"As soon as I'm better, baby," she says, "and the doctors say that I'm getting just a little bit better every day."

Warwick Penitentiary, A-Block
1995

"Gimme the spoon, Dershowitz," Big Doug says. An officer, he gets twice the respect of the other ranks just on account of his size.

"Give him the damn spoon, Dershowitz," some guard orders.

"We'll take your recreational privileges," Big Doug reminds him. "We'll take your outdoor privileges..." He pauses, to let it all sink in. "If you get a real bad report, they might put you in lockdown."

"Shut up! They're not gonna put anybody in lockdown. Look. All's I want is the bathrooms cleaned so I don't get nobody's clap." Dershowitz got himself entwined with the bars and his torn orange jumper. Somewhere in the tangle of flesh and metal is a spoon.

"Look, man," Big Doug says, confidentially. "Ain't nobody getting ass up in here. And if you lucky, nobody's gettin' into your junk neither."

"There're microbes. There're bugs. They get on my clothes; they get on my hair. I just want clean toilets, then I'll give up the spoon."

"Give it up. Give it to me. Just give it up, just give it. Give it up..."

This is what I have to listen to, as I lay on the thin plastic mattress; when I drift off, my thoughts are full of it. The ceiling above is gray, cracking. The average tone of metals, especially when the lye has worn them down to a dull luster, is gray. Faces look gray. Eyes. It must be spreading.

"You too, Wonicki," Big Doug says, to me, when they finally force the spoon out of his fingers, as though there'd even been something to you-too me about.

And when I wake up, Dershowitz is gone but Big Doug is still trolling the block, though the lights have shut down and all the cells are quiet.

I pull up in front of the suburban ranch, kicking the curb with rubber. I never could parallel park. A rotweiler is snapping at the air behind a fence. I ding the bell and rap on the door, because I don't own a key. Carla opens up and goes right away to sit on the sectional sofa. That's like our place. We sit on those torn-up pieces of couch and bullshit all night, or we smoke and play gin, poker; sometimes I come over and she's already crying and she won't stop until she's asleep.

"I heard you were, like, pregnant," I say.

"Yeah," she says, as though it's a passing affliction.

"Is it Angel's baby?" I ask.

She laughs, crooked.

"What?" I try to read her face.

"You think I'm a hooker or something?" She says.

"No, no. Carla, I was just..."

"Don't worry. He asked me the same thing."

My temples flare. I can feel the tension in my skull. "Why? Does he think we're..." I gesture.

She laughs again, but it's a snotty, tear-welling laugh.

"Apparently, someone's been saying..."

She's too full of fluids to go on. I scan around for a tissue or something. Ashtray. Remote. TV Guide.

"What?" I feel a pang in my side, as if my apprehensions wielded knives.

"That...I'm, like, your personal fuck toy and that, like, we do it all the time and shit like that." She looked up from under her hair.

"Who said...?" Looking at her—really looking at her now—I notice the welt on her cheekbone, and a red mark where her neck meets her shoulder. "Did Angel...?"

A thumping at the door. The rotweiler picks up the rhythm.

"Shit, he's here." Carla's tears seem to harden on her face like wax.

"You don't have to answer it. He doesn't know you're home," I suggest.

"I'm gonna let him in," she says.

29

"Don't do that," I insist.

"I'm gonna let him in."

I look around the room again, this time for something blunt and heavy. Instead, I settle on a fork that's still sticky with syrup. I palm it uneasily.

Angel busts in looking pumped, revved up. I remind myself to be calm, but as he advances, I raise the fork above my head like a knife-wielding maniac in a horror flick—and suddenly there's a snap in my ear, and Angel is lying on the floor, and blood is easing from a wound in his side. A second shot. I look over at Carla, and she's holding the pistol unsteadily, drooping from her two hands while her face turns the other way. Under her tank top, I notice for the first time a very slight bulge in her belly.

"Look at me," I say, a few times, before it registers. "Look at me...Look at me." By the time she looks up, it's like hours have passed. We can already hear the sirens sounding in our heads.

Angel lets out a faint croak, and his spasms become more infrequent. I snatch the gun from Carla, and it loosens easily from her skeletal grip. I rub it down with my shirt and, holding it steady in my hand, like a joystick, I sit on the edge of our sofa and wait.

WASTE MANAGEMENT, INDIA POINT
1997

The boy is laying flat on the sidewalk, fresh from a bicycle accident, when we pass by on our route. I motion the driver to stop, then hop off and sit beside him. He says he's hurt, but the only thing I can see is scrapes on one shin. "Whatchado?" I ask.

"I tried to pop a wheelie," he says, "from the curb." His talk strains, like he's constipated.

"You weren't thinking," I say, as if reporting the facts.

"I flew for a couple of seconds," he says. "I was like, whooosh."

"I'm not getting you another bike. You better take care of this one."

I help him sit up, like he's a convalescent patient. "Can I have something to drink, pop?"

It's just like Tony to milk a weakness. I fish out an energy bar from my jacket pocket. From GNC. "How's this, Tony? Bueno?"

"Si. Bueno."

We share our meal replacement bar, chewing alone in our separate sensations. For a second there, I think we're about to share a good silent moment. Then he asks, "Do you ever feel bad about Mom?"

"Why?" I say, keeping it light.

"That she crazy?"

I clear my throat. I try not to look at him. "That's nobody's fault, Tony."

He's still looking at me. He's got a big forehead, and dark eyes, like Angel.

"Yeah, well. That's all I have to say."

WARWICK PENITENTIARY, A-BLOCK
1996

They let me out on a Wednesday. It's too late in the week to go looking for a job, and too early to relax or settle in. But Carla's pop—Tony's grandpa—knows what happened, and sets me up with a job in his department: the department of sanitation.

From the back of a truck, I graduate to sales, though I'm still dealing in trash. Nothing essential has changed—just the job description, to which new lines are added every day I show up for work, it seems like. I used to just pick it up and pass it on. Now I sell it.

There are companies that buy the shit you throw away. Or, if they do business with the wrong people, we make 'em buy it. Point is, we get it from you for free. Then we sell it as many times as we can, cleaning money from other sources. Then more money comes in for us to dump it—tax money, anyway. So what it all amounts to is billing. Accounts payable. Invoices. Receipts. Eventually, I guess, I'll be just another broker.

But at the moment, we've got the truck stopped at a SpeedMart, because I have a bitter taste on my tongue—probably from the fumes—and I need a dose of sugar. I fill a handcart with chewy, colorful candy, and step in line. Next to me, a revolving display case reads "frames for all occasions." Some are wiry and fragile, for light

31

use. And others are heavy, sturdy, made for rough climates.

But sunglasses only come in one color now—dark. The John Lennon look is dead as disco. But I know for a fact that that color wheel still hangs in the art room of my old high school. I went there once when I got out. No particular reason. I was just a kid when they put me in, and it was the only place I really knew. When I did, I noticed that, while all the rest of the colors are out at the edges, gray is in the middle of the wheel. As it turns out, the opposite of gray is...just gray. So you can look through gray glasses your whole life if you want, and when you turn your eyes back onto what's around you, instead of seeing something different—some new quality of light—all you see is more gray.

PROVIDENCE PUBLIC HIGH SCHOOL, TRUANT 1986

When he's got me in the back of the car with cuffs on, he wants to know how young I am. That's how he says it, "How young are you?" I just turned eighteen. He whistles, but you can tell it's a practiced whistle. Back at the station, he wants to know if I'm a lefty. Like he wants me to pitch for little league.

When I get up the courage, I ask him, "What'll it be, do you think?"

He looks grim. "Manslaughter. Ten to twenty." Casually, he dispenses with a decade or two of my life.

"Guess I'll never be President," I say. He snorts. Then I wonder how many times he's heard that. I'd hate to be a typical arrest, another day-in-the-life.

At forty, I'll practically be an old man. Carla will have been a mom for twenty years—her kid will be older than I am now. And Angel will still be eighteen and dead. As I'm brought to the station, and as they process me, and for a while afterwards, I actually envy Angel—I envy him, and envy him, until enough time goes by and I don't envy him anymore.

Four Hundred and One

James Mason

1

James had been watching the paperboy for months. It was summer, and the first time since 1971, according to his ledger, that the newspaper had been delivered to his door by a kid on a bike. The bike was a blue Shwinn, with a banana seat and a carriage on the back, holding a neighborhood-worth of newsprint, wrapped in pink rubberbands or stuffed into plastic bags for protection from the weather. The kid was a war refugee, it occurred to James, one of the Southeast Asians he read about in the papers—a straight line of black hair across his forehead; eyes like barely-cracked walnuts.

"How strange," thought James, "for a kid like that to go out and deliver the news, which is written about him."

One day James caught the boy testing the doorknob. James was watching him through the pinhole when, instead of tossing the paper onto the stoop and passing the house, he walked up to the door and knocked. Then knocked again. His head pressed up against the door, James could feel the vibration in the wood. Then the doorknob, which was securely locked, jangled uselessly. Finding himself in such proximity with a foreigner, and always a little unsure how to act among strangers, James began to bark like an angry dog, which succeeded in frightening the boy away.

2

"One motion, each moment," James had to remind himself, to spare him another day of remaining in bed, turning his head back and forth, eyes scanning the walls for slight variations of line and color, from which to decipher hidden meanings.

The ceiling fan stopped working months ago. The air flow in the house was static, so that the dust particles seemed paralyzed in zero-gravity—suspended by invisible electric currents, or by the

33

very rays of light that reveal them, angled and warm through the unclean glass. And James remembered reading that, according to certain physical laws, if motion is slowed, then time must be slowed too—almost to the point of pause. It was this aura of stillness in the house that convinced James never to get a television, the flow of which mechanism, James thought, might one day be reversed so that instead of giving him having access to the world, it would have access to him.

3

Another thing that James' ledger reported that day was a visit from the meter reader—a woman—the first since he began keeping his record thirty-one years ago. And of course, the usual appearance of the mailman (male, hispanic, trimmed mustache), and the trash man (Russian or Polish, thirty-something, dirty-blonde, thick-bodied). The year before, a census-taker visited this house, and was so persistent that James finally opened his door to her. The questions confused him—set him off on mental digressions so far from the original line of inquiry that he could barely respond at all. "Are you the owner of this home?" would bring back memories of its purchase in 1954, before they put in the highway, and the young expecting couple who sold it to him, before moving away to a larger house in the suburbs. The question, "How many people live in this household?" would set James to wondering who else might be living there with him undetected—Why does she ask such questions? Does she know something I don't?

Sometimes it seemed to James, through the ever-narrowing pinhole on his front door, that he was visited by a thousand changing uniforms, and inside those uniforms, no person. Or as if it were the same person changing outfits, and that ghost-bureaucrat kept coming back to check up on him several times a day—to report on his whereabouts and activities, which never changed.

4

To keep the body busy—to subdue it into the unconscious activity of the everyday—James had learned to whittle. It was one thing that his nerves could do without being told. Everything else had to be uttered, commanded—"lift the skillet" (to an arm), "spread the oil in the pan by slowly rotating" (to the wrist), "release handle" (to the fingers). There is memory in the hands—James remembered reading somewhere—that survives the severest blow to the head. But, like all other forms of memory, it is selective, and biased towards what we wish were true.

James had recently lost the ability to focus his thoughts on reading books, or writing them, which since retiring from the Navy had been his only preoccupation. So whittling had become the cipher of his old age. As far as writing went, he could now only collect and record bits of data. His brain, hand, and pen did not work in harmony. But the whittling knife made sense.

Living as he did along the canal that divides the Downcity from the East Side, James whittled mostly model ships. In three days, on the anniversary of his father's death, James planned to go outside and let the small fleet sail down the water to its tributary.

Together with his father and uncles—long dead now—James' family had given fifty-five years to the navy. James' father had spent his old age trying to take back those years, to wrest from the government the restitution he was owed for the sacrifice of his leg to a "friendly" mine during the first world war (with which undertaking he frequently occupied himself in times when James was in his care).

As for James himself, he grew up fully aware of how much greater a sacrifice his father and uncles had made, and with a persistent feeling that he himself owed much more to the Navy than he had given.

James worked as an off-base decoder for the Navy during World War II. In those years, every division of the military had its own intelligence unit, with very little communication between them. James' team consisted of himself and two other men, both of whom, like James himself, were quiet and solitary. One of the officers, who they called Vance, was so fat that James wondered how he got into the Navy, and who James never recalled seeing without his spectacles; the other officer, Larsen, grew a short-cropped, red beard, in defiance of Navy regulations, and mumbled to himself. Together, yet alone, the three cryptologists sat hunched at their stations working out solutions to problems created by the Japanese. Occasionally, it would occur to James that a cryptologist is the student of his enemy—the teacher knows the answer, but a student must work it out on his own. Though, in this case, if the formula he sought was found, it could save men's lives. Before long, Larsen's mumbling would stop sounding to James like code and begin to sound like prayer.

5

The next day, James opened the shutters of his window, and looked out while the trash man emptied the bin into his truck, and moved on. As the sound of the trash truck faded into the distance, James looked upon the day as if to say, "You're here, and I'm here, and we might as well just get used to each other."

The sunlight was scattershot through the walnut tree on his small square of lawn; forming scintillating patterns as it passed through the blinds. James heeded the advice he'd heard since he was a boy, not to look directly at the sun. He whittled instead, whittled until his hands were tired, until the sun no longer shone through the East window, until the wood in his hands was smooth as glass.

The paperboy had come back that day with a slice of beef jerky between his fingers. He had knocked, and when no answer came, not even a sigh or whimper, he left the wrinkled meat on the mat outside the door. When James went to pick up the paper that afternoon, he saw the sliver of meat on the mat, and stared down at it like a line of code to be interpreted.

6

James finished another ship, cut out of a fresh panel of wood. Hollow, narrow, canoe-like, this ship might have been designed for speed. Most of the boats were shallow, given the quality and type of wood he had to use; but every tenth attempt or so, he built a frigate that could have sailed for the British Navy. Cursed with a seaman's superstition, which turned any suggestion of ease into an omen of ill-luck, he appraised his latest creation with modest regard. "I guess she's seaworthy," he said. "She'll take to the river, anyway."

With her sharp, ridged contours and plashy complexion, James thought, she was not the prettiest ship to float on water, but she would make it out to the Atlantic, and perhaps, further. He named her "Sinker." In Japan, James recalled hearing, mothers do not praise their children, because they fear that evil spirits will overhear and take the good child for their own.

James held onto the knob for a long while before turning it and opening it outward into the light.

Whenever James passed through the threshold of his house into the open world, even in the summer, he felt slightly cold, as though the architecture of his house were another layer of clothes that he were shedding. Denuded, James walked down the hill from his house, to the Main Street canal, in a gray church-suit, a belt and pin with the Navy insignia, and a white fedora hat.

When James was young, gentlemen still wore hats. Wearing a hat was a sign that you were humble before God. In a courtroom, or at a funeral, removing your hat meant that you understood the gravity of the place. But in the city, where you saw a head go bare, there were sure to be ten more with hats upon them and faces underneath that scowled at the gall of it. From his red colonial on Benefit Street, James watched as the generations lost their sense of modesty, the way a child might lose a shoe but hobble on, indifferent to its lack.

James' only contact was a sister-in-law, Nancy. James frequently thought of her as still a teenager, because she was only fifteen when they met, in 1942. Her sister—James' wife—Helen, was seven years her senior. And when he thought of Nancy, he still thought of her as a precocious child, full of coyness and curiosity. Nancy made a point of visiting James once a year, meeting him at the pier on August 8th, for the boat ritual.

"Oh. You," James said, spotting Nancy in his peripheral vision.

"Yeah, 'oh, you' too," said Nancy, putting a hand on his shoulder and stroking it gently.

James pulled his arm away jerkily. "Helen isn't home. Come back later; she'll probably be around," he said.

"She's dead," Nancy said. "Been dead twenty-eight years to the day."

James laughed. "That's what I keep telling her; but they won't let her go at the office. They need her there, almost much as I do. Damn, if Helen left now, they wouldn't know where to find their own thumbs."

If James were looking in Nancy's direction, he would have seen her wrinkled eyes and freckled face dropping, her chin settling on the chest.

Looking vaguely in her direction, James added, "Maybe she should ask for a raise."

"Jean wants to see you again," Nancy said. "I told her, 'What's the point?' but she wants to come see for herself. She's stubborn, like her father."

Now James frowned, as though a part of him understood. "Helen will take care of Jean."

James had met Helen the day he finished college, and he understood then that it would be his last day with her before heading for duty in the Navy. So they talked and held hands in the quad until the sun went down, and before they knew it the sun came back up the next day, and James spent his first week as an officer sleep-deprived, feeling cold and hot at the same time—sweaty and thirsty, but with no appetite at all.

Helen, on the other hand, was just about to get a head start on her second year by taking summer classes at Providence College, but knew with a stoic certainty that now she would not be able to finish her studies—because she would, inevitably, marry the lovestruck soldier.

"You guys were so lovey-dovey, it made everyone sick," Nancy said. "I mean, sick. You guys were disgusting."

"Nobody forced you to spy on us," James returned.

"How else was I supposed to learn? We didn't own a TV."

Their first and only pregnancy was twins. Twin girls. They named the older one Mae and the younger, Jean. But the first one died before she left the womb, and the second one lived, but complications from her birth caused Helen to suffer liver failure, and death.

"I realized," Nancy said, "that you only knew Helen for four years before she passed away. It's weird; I mean, four years is nothing. You practically didn't even know her."

James smiled like it hurt.

"I know Helen better than I know anything," he said.

Nancy looked into his profile. Unlike James, she could not see the young man underneath the old one. "That's not saying much," she said.

The water plunked against the sides of the pier, echoing underneath. The sun was slowly approaching the water horizon.

James opened the paper bag in which he kept his fleet of small ships, and pulled them out one at a time and ceremoniously pushed each one out to sea. They looked, at the sunset-moment into which James had quite accidentally stumbled, like real ships; and the sky, like fake sky.

"There's no way of saying it without sounding cruel," Nancy began, "but maybe it's time for you to move on; you know, find someone else who fulfills you in the same way. It's never too late to start over."

Nancy thought that, perhaps, in the dead space between her earnest platitudes and James' response, her words may have found traction in the inner James, the one she had not seen for several years. Then, abruptly, James let out a fierce laugh that, after a few moments, turned into a cough.

"Do you remember when you used to give her those timepieces?" Nancy asked him. "For her birthday, Christmas, Easter, her graduation…"

"Of course," James said, watching the object of so many hours of his devotion disappear into the distance. "She collected them."

"No, James. She never did."

James stood silently until the ships crowned the limit of his vision and were gone.

When he got back, James felt a slight disturbance in the permanence of the room. A breeze, unlike the calm he usually felt in the study. An open window jostled the blinds, making the louvers click against each other in a faint staccato. He looked up to meet the face of the paperboy, silhouetted by an azure sky, with neat rows of hair and peat-brown eyes. "Hi," he said, with casual aplomb, as if spying on old men were a fashionable thing to do.

James took a long moment convincing himself that the boy's presence was, in fact, material rather than theoretical. James was troubled by the boy's face, marked with the pox, and utterly unreadable. He could be thinking anything, James thought, narrowing his eyes in unconscious imitation of the boy.

"Where's your dog?" the boy asked, passing a biscuit from hand to hand, which motion, for what reason James could not fully apprehend, made his own hands feel suddenly weary and sore. "I thought you had a dog," he says.

Knowing only that he wanted him to go away, James began to bark.

8

James collected phone directories from around the country. Sometimes, James looked up other James Masons, added them up, determined what percentages they accounted for in their region— always statistically insignificant, falling somewhere between .0001 and .0004 nationwide. He reported this data in his ledger. James was still missing directories from twelve states, a total of thirty-four area codes to go.

James' area code, 401, was an important number, he thought, a prime number; the sum of the first and last letters of the Hebrew alphabet; the number that occurs most frequently in the Christian Bible; the number of deities in the pantheon of the Orisha tribe of West Africa (who are referred to as "the four hundred and the one"—the many and the only); the number found on the hull of the Titanic—a ship on which many passengers bound for Providence had walked, talked, and dined, but never arrived.

As he lay down in bed that night, James' mind wound its coils around the thought of his wife, in this city, those days. In the Navy, James spent much of his time with maps. They often drew circles on the maps—the radii of locations where a communiqué was intercepted, or in which a foreign object was spotted. They drew circles, and circles around the circles, to suggest degrees of distance from the center. On his cerebral map, as sleep dropped, James drew four-dimensional circles around Helen in the year 1942, in the city of Providence.

9

James noticed the paperboy crouching on the sidewalk across the street, looking between the cracks at something tiny. The boy was talking to himself, in another language. He thought of Larsen.

James went out the door and crossed the unlined street. "What are you doing here?" James asked the boy.

"I live here," the kid said, pointing to the house behind him—the one across the street from James'.

That's impossible, James thought, a missionary and his wife live in that house. Or was that a long time ago? "Don't you go to school?"

"It's summer," the kid said.

He had an answer for everything, James thought. He's a clever one. "Why are you always coming up to my door?"

"I deliver the paper," the boy said. Then, "and my mother asked me to meet everyone in the neighborhood and to greet them."

James bristled at this. So, his parents sent him out to spy for them. "But why?"

"The only people my parents know are people who live far away." He was standing now, his head still looking down at the sidewalk. His English was suspiciously good, though heavily accented. "They want me to meet all the neighbors, but no one is home all day but you."

James stood quietly.

"Why are you taking your house apart?" the boy asked, pointing across the street, to where James' house, from this distance, appeared full of holes—foot-sized gaps in the wooden structure that gave it the appearance of being chewed at slowly from the inside. One hole had grown so large that you could see the frame, which itself had been carved out of—whittled into small ships that were, by now, floating lazily down to the ocean, or sunk. "Are you building something?"

But James did not hear what the boy was saying now. His mind was circling around something that the boy had said earlier. How did it go? My parents know people who live far away...People live far away...The only people are people who live far away...My parents are people who live far away...?

10

James' ledger had a light brown cover, tape-bound, cracked in the middle as though the whole book had been frequently folded. The yellowed pages were covered in tiny perfect letters, which grew larger and more awkward as one leafed through it, until, at the end, it appeared as though someone had simply broken pencils over the page and let the book close over the graphite dust.

When he met his daughter Jean for the first time, she was twenty, and a student at college. She had always believed that Nancy and David were her natural parents, and was awestruck when she learned that her hermit uncle was really her father. She pretended that she had to interview him for a History class, and he went along with it, because he felt that he owed her something. She asked him about his life, his tragic marriage, and his years in the Navy; James hesitated before telling her that he killed no one, that he saved no one, and that he never did quite enough in his capacity as an officer or a husband.

The next time he met Jean, it was after he underwent emergency heart surgery, and she came to the hospital to make peace with him before he could die. She confessed her anger, she thanked him for bringing her into the world, but let him know that she wanted so much more from him than what he had given her. She cried and beat her chest. She wrung her hands as though they were wet clothes to be strung up.

But if James could hear her speaking, he showed no hint of it. Instead, he looked down into his lap, at his own hands, which were, to his surprise, old man hands.

Manhunt

Kate Waltham

The house is trashed again. I would say it looks like a tornado struck, except that, if anything, the junk looks like it belongs to the room—as though it has grown there, straight from the carpet, and no one has the right to remove it from its own ecology. After a few hours, I could have it passably neat again, but the price of cleanliness is constant war with the tendency of unstable objects to fall to the ground. And this time, as every time, I experience a moment of hesitation a seductive rush of laissez-faire—when I tilt my face up toward the track-lighting and ask, "why bother?"

In the sixties and seventies, my family lived in a 40-acre plot outside of Newport, and we went through cleaning ladies like baskets of laundry, but then the market fell. We moved here, to this tragedy-proof suburb, where I still feel displaced among the middle-income moms with their playground politics and their Jane Austen book clubs. For months after we moved, I felt like a tenement-dweller, and even cried occasionally (though not in front of Morton), because there is nothing like cleaning your own house to make a girl feel like the Cinderella who never found her prince and is now riding in the pumpkin-carriage of middle-age.

Tuesday is officially the solstice, and Emma is preparing for the first slumber party of the season. I'm scared for her, because she's so innocent (and I know that all mother's think this—but I don't know how many mothers know their daughters as well as I know mine), and girls today are so…not innocent. If I had more time to worry, I'd probably come around and be excited for her—expanding as she is beyond her usual one-friend-at-a-time arrangement. Her bosom-buddy Lou will be here too, but she'll go away to live with her dad in Phoenix in a week, and Emma will be at the mercy of "the group."

If I had even more time to think about it, I would probably forego the party, forbid friends from coming over at all, and become the neighborhood Boo Radley. But the way things are, I can think of nothing else—I can do nothing else—but just go on picking up

45

one piece of junk at a time until the house is ready for the girls to come over and "slumber" (because if you called it a "sleeping party," I guess, no one would bother).

Emma Waltham

Lou gets here first, and that's all right, since we know how to talk to each other, and she never really tries to make me uncomfortable. But I'm also a little upset that she came early, because I told her the party was at 6 and Why does she think she can come early just because she used to come over all the time when we were little? When Jen and Shayna come over it'll seem like Lou was here the whole time—like she lives here or something—as though we were just here all alone at my house, playing.

Lou makes me mad sometimes, but then—if I didn't invite her?—my God, she'd probably hit me or something—she's kind of a tomboy, if you can't tell by her name, which is Louisiana, but even so, Wouldn't you go by "Louise" or "Lois" or even "Anna"? Her mom lives alone—I mean, not alone, but just with her kids—and when anyone asks her what she does, she just sighs and says "freelance," which as far as I can tell means playing solitaire and reading romance novels. Point is, Lou doesn't like being at home, so she comes over all the time, which was fun for a while, but now things are feeling kind of crowded. It's not like Lou lives here.

Lucky for me, Lou goes right upstairs to talk with my sister Dierdre, who she totally idolizes. Lou knows I'm mad (I forgot to say that Lou is a mind-reader), so she leaves me to wait on the steps, which makes me even more mad, left with nothing but my frustration and no one to direct it at. I don't know why I get so mad sometimes (I refuse to accept the "time of the month" explanation dad gives), but when I do, I use a "coping strategy" my mother taught me: draw a picture of the thing you are mad at, then tear it up into tiny pieces.

Jennifer Aldiss

I can see Emma through the window, and I can see that she sees me walking up to the door, so why does she make me knock? Like

I'm just dying to go to her party. But whatever, I knock and she opens it just in time to see Shayna Zimmerman and Mrs. Z pull up too. I turn around to watch Shayna walk up to the door—Emma hasn't even said "hi" to me yet—and then Mrs. Z and my mom get out of their vans and start talking with their arms folded, even though the sun is about to set and *Hello,* this is a *slumber* party.

Shayna says "hi" and walks inside, but I'm out here watching our moms chatting. "Ma, go home!" I call out, finally. And she just waves like she can't hear me.

Mrs. Waltham is in the kitchen, putting out paper plates and cups, napkins, and plastic forks and knives. When the pizza man comes, my Mom and Mrs. Z are still at it, probably talking about us, even though the sun has set over the trees. Mrs. Waltham half-smiles and half-nods out at the other moms when she picks up the pizza with one hand, pays with the other, and looks at me strange. "Jen, honey, what are doing still waiting outside? Come on in."

Mrs. Waltham is weird about food. I mean, she orders us pizza, then she walks in later and snickers at us. "You kids with your pizza," she says, like she'd offered us a salad and we asked for pizza instead. Then while we are getting set up in the living room, she comes in to offer us the last uneaten slices of pizza that were sitting in the box, like she can't stand to have leftovers. Her house is so neat, it's ridiculous. And she's always checking in on us, like she wants to catch us doing something wrong, or she wants to join us or something. I don't know which is worse.

As long as Mrs. Waltham is around, we can only do kid stuff, like trivial pursuit (which is boring) or put on a kid's movie.

But then, when we set up our movie, first Shayna makes us wait while she goes to the bathroom, and then, after we start the movie, she goes to the bathroom again. When she comes back she just sits down and says, "What'd I miss?"

Just the whole movie, Shayna, that's all. I say, "What were doing that whole time in the bathroom?"

Shayna hides under her hair, totally silent as the movie plays on.

The Last Unicorn is what we're watching, and it's the part when the horse—I mean, "Unicorn"—is turned into a human woman by the wizard. She looks like an albino, which right away makes me think of Danny from school. "Do you guys think Danny Oren is cute?" I ask them.

"I think Danny is sweet," Shayna says.

"Danny is really sweet," says Emma.

"Yeah, but do you think he's cute?" I want to know.

"Why? Because you think he's cute?" Lou says.

The way she talks is like she's above it all. "No-o," I say, by reflex (what else can you say when someone asks you that?).

"What's your definition of cute?" Lou asks. She's so analytical, even about boys. "Who is cute, in your opinion?"

"Jared Hennesy," I blurt, like a moron.

Lou scoffs. "That's so typical," she says.

"Come on. Jared is the hottest guy in the school. You can't say he isn't," Shayna says, trying to be helpful.

Lou says, "Yes I can. Watch: Jared Hennesy isn't the hottest guy in school." I don't know why I should care what Lou thinks. She's so drab, she never has anything nice to say, and she looks Mexican to me.

"I bet if he asked, you would go out with him," I said.

Lou stops, like she's having deep thoughts, and says, "yeah, I probably would." All our faces light up with the opportunity presented.

"I mean, if anyone wanted to go out with me so bad that they'd come up and ask me, I'd try going out with them. Once, I mean." But we might as well not have been listening. Emma's already got the phone and calling Jared.

Emma holds out the phone too long, and we hear a muted operator voice: If you'd like to make a call, please hang up and try again. Shayna hangs up the phone with a finger. "Wait. Are we going to prank call him? Or is Lou going to ask him out?"

"I didn't say I wanted to ask him out," Lou says.

"Okay, we'll prank him."

Louisiana Frick

Shayna was in my third period study hall this year, so I've had a lot of time to think about why I don't like her. The main thing is that she flirts all the time, which, okay, I might do too if I had her confidence, but then it's like, when there are no boys around, she doesn't know what to do with herself. When she's around other girls, she just talks about the boys who, I'd bet, she'd rather be flirting with. And, to be totally honest, she's not even that pretty—I should know, I had to look at her face for forty-five minutes, five days a week, for a hundred and eighty days. It's just that she's small-featured and blonde and smiles a lot, and—you know what?—some people just can't go around smiling all the time because after a while your face hurts.

And, I'm sorry, but Jen is dumb, and ugly too. She's got broad shoulders like a man and really dry red hair that feels like a horse's. The only thing going for her is she's loud, and the only good it does is that she's dumb at higher volumes. When the movie ends, she insists that we watch *Poltergeist*, which she says is scarier than *The Exorcist*, which as far as I'm concerned is only scary because of the music.

Then, when we're done with *Poltergeist*, Jen insists on watching MTV, which I'll be the first to admit I watch at home, but is such a boring thing to do when you get a group of people together and claim to be having a "party." We should be doing...I don't know, something else.

Shayna agrees with me on this point, so we're brainstorming what to do. Everything we can think of involves going outside, but Emma says forget it, we're not allowed to go outside tonight. "But c'mon," I say, "Kate won't mind if we just go out on the deck, right?" Emma scowls at me, and I'm not sure whether it's because I'm challenging the rule of the house, or because I called her mom "Kate." "What do you think, Shayna? What should we do?" Shayna gets straight A's on her report cards, but when you ask her to come up with an idea, she just goes blank like a mannequin. Which is why I'd really rather just be hanging out with Emma, who is quiet and not flirty and has an original idea of her own now and then. Her sister Dierdre is awesome, and she lets us use her video camera—she used to orchestrate these dance numbers with Emma and me that, now that I think about it, I dread the idea of Jen finding and putting on the TV for everyone to see.

But then a Madonna video comes on and Shayna says, "Guys,

49

what about *Truth or Dare?*" and I say, "sure, why not," because the whole idea of the game is to convince the other players that you have nothing to hide.

Shayna Zimmerman

"You go first," Lou says, and I'm surprised, and a little hurt too since we'd just recently struck up this alliance—the let's-do-something-else-besides-watch-TV-alliance.

"Fine," I say. "Truth."

"All right," Lou says, smiling, "what were you doing in the bathroom?"

Shit. Either tell or don't tell. Make a decision quick. Truth. The rules of the game are binding. "I was feeling sick after all that pizza, so I had to throw up."

"Wow, that's more truth than I wanted," Lou says.

"Eww," Jen says, "Shayna threw up in your bathroom," like Emma didn't hear me in the first place.

"Okay, you're turn, Lou," I say, wanting to deflect the attention away as quick as possible.

"Truth," Lou says.

I'm quiet for a long time. I hadn't thought of a follow-up question. Then I remembered *Poltergeist.* "What is the most scared you've ever been, and why?"

The girls laugh, and Jen grumbles over how easy the question is.

"Okay," says Lou, "it was when Ken and I were visiting our dad a couple summers ago. His place in Arizona was new—one of the rooms wasn't even completely built yet. My dad was out, I don't remember why, maybe on a date or something, and Ken was babysitting me. We got into this huge fight, and I just left—I ran away, until I got so far away I realized that I had no idea where I was."

"You were scared because you were lost?" Jen sneers.

"I'd be scared," Emma suggests.

"Yeah, me too," says Jen, "if I were a baby!"

"Well, you guys asked," Lou says, with a shrug. "My dad lives way out in the desert, and when it's dark in the desert, and there's no one but you and the snakes, you get scared."

"Well, that's the first you said anything about snakes," Jen says.

"I didn't see the snakes, but I knew they were there, which is worse."

Everyone picks Truth. From the way we throw it around, you'd think Truth was cheap. It gets to a point where Dare is almost taboo. What are we so afraid of? What's the worst Dare there is? Maybe you'd have to drink pee or something.

Finally, it's Emma's turn. "Dare," she says, with a wicked grin, knowing the reaction she's guaranteed to get. And we don't disappoint her.

Jen chooses the Dare. "Okay, okay. I dare you to go outside and take a walk around the block alone."

"No, no," we all say at the same time.

"I told you, I'm not allowed to go outside tonight," Emma huffs.

"That's the game," Jen says.

"Hey," says Lou, "How about Emma still has to do her Dare, but we all go out with her? And Dierdre comes too."

"What kind of a Dare is that?" Jen says, and I actually agree with her.

Dierdre Waltham

I'm barely awake when I realize I'm outside walking on a sidewalk in the dark, with Emma and her friends. They're all bunched together like a bouquet, and the wind is muffling the sound of nervous girl-chatter. Nervous because scared, I guess—though I don't know what all the fuss is about. This neighborhood is about as safe as our living room; I often find myself wishing it were less "safe"—wishing there were a good reason for us to stay inside all day—not just because we're bored.

Still groggy with sleep, I only register a part of what is going on around me, I can only process sound-bytes. "Maybe we should tell ghost stories?"; "I Dare someone to scream at the top of their lungs"; "Are we still playing the game?"; "How about we just walk half the block, and then go back?"; "That's the same distance, stupid!"; "Isn't it against the law to be out after midnight?"

"Calm down, guys, it's not like we're in the ghetto or anything,"

I say. "This is Rhode Island."

"My brother says that there are gangs in Rhode Island, though. Like, lot's of 'em," Lou says.

"Yeah, I heard that the big-time gangsters came from Rhode Island," Jen says.

"Oh, sure. Maybe the Shriners," I say.

"I don't care. I think we should go home," Shayna says.

"What, are you really scared?" says Jen.

"Jesus, guys, you're the ones who brought me out here, now let's just go around the stupid block." Just as I say so, a car passes slowly, and I swear I can feel the eyes of the passengers staring out. The other girls feel it too, because they go quiet suddenly, and huddle in closer.

Fear stinks. I used to think it was a metaphor. "The smell of fear." No. It's a genuine stink. Sweat and glands and oil. Around these shifty thirteen-year olds, I smell it everywhere.

But we're saved when another car appears off in the distance, heading toward us, and the first one speeds off. It's funny. One car: scary. Two cars: not so scary.

Kenneth Frick

No moon, nothin'. Just the brand-new striping on the road. I wonder why they bother with the new asphalt and paint here in Warwick when the really busy streets down in Providence are full of potholes. Angell—who knows everything there is to know about the police—says that, in the City of Providence Public Works Department, it's somebody's job to go around with a sledgehammer, putting holes in the streets and sidewalks, so that the local concrete company is guaranteed a contract. I don't know if I believe that, but you can't argue with shitty roads.

Which makes it all the sweeter out here with the windows rolled down and Angell coasting 25 miles above the limit, looking for someone's party to crash—a place to get wasted in peace, without having to explain yourself to anybody.

Up ahead, there's a group of girls—I mean, girly-girls, dressed in pink tops and yellow shorts and so on. "Slow down," I say. "Hotties on the prowl." We down-shift to a crawl. Approaching them at this speed, it's obvious what's what.

"Dude, they're like twelve years old," Angell says, letting out a wicked laugh. "Ken wants to bag himself a prepube."

"Shut the fuck up, man. You thought they were hotties too," I say.

"No way, man. I don't go for that. You know how long you could go to jail for that shit? And do you know what they do to pedophiles in State prison?" Angell won't let up.

"I'm seventeen. Tell me how I'm a fuckin' pedophile?" I sulk against the window.

"Don't get all defensive, man," Angell says, and we ride quietly.

"Hey, Angell," I say, "isn't that D.W.?" Dierdre Waltham is a sophomore (was a sophomore) and a "9" according to our yearbook fuckability rating system.

"Hey, Kenny," Angell says, leaning on the wheel, pointing us in their direction. "Isn't that your sister?"

Sure enough, Lou is standing in this gaggle of girls—the only earth tone in what looks like the hot-pink field-hockey team.

"Yup, that's her."

Angell flips on the brights, and the gang of freshmen-to-be are thrust into a white spotlight. "Let's scare the shit out of them," he says, and steps on the gas. I mean, you can *hear him* step on the gas.

Angell Ramon

The car fuckin' lands on the grass. The curb has the slightest bit of incline, which sends the car a foot or two in the air before coming down with a jiggle like Dukes of Fuckin' Hazard, on a lawn ten feet shy of the slumber party in motion. I'm laughing my brains out, but Ken goes to unclick his seatbelt. Our hearts are pumping stereo-loud, like club music. The girls scatter so fast I don't even have a chance to kill the engine. For some reason, I didn't expect they would bolt like that. Stupid, I know, but I guess in my head I thought they'd freeze up, "like a deer in headlights," because a twelve-year-old girl is the closest thing you'll get to a deer in the suburbs.

Ken pops the handle and steps out, running into the space where the girls used to be, calling out hopelessly, "Guys, come on out! We were just kidding!" After a few minutes of that, he returns to the car and leans in the driver's side window, like he's gonna fuckin' give me directions. "That was messed up, man. Why'd you do that?"

"Relax, man. Get back in the car."

When Ken is back in the bitch seat, we pull around the block with the lights off, and park.

"I'm telling you, those girls are gonna run straight home and call the cops," Ken says.

Cops don't like me. It's mutual, as far as I'm concerned, but there's something about me that rubs them the wrong way. Sometimes I wonder if it's a race thing, but whatever, it doesn't even matter, the main thing is that I avoid cops. Ever since I was arrested for arson, when I was a kid, I've had one eye out for the blue and red. I bought a police scanner, a tracking radar, and a handgun (which, because my mom would kick my ass if she found it, I keep at my girlfriend Carla's house).

I think about the Waltham house, a block and a half ahead. I think about the Warwick Police Station, a mile down the road. I think about the 48 hours I spent there, at fifteen, when I just barely escaped a six-month tour of juvie. I think about those little girls hiding in the dark, who I'll bet are smart enough to take down my car's plates. I imagine how stupid it would be to finally get stuck in jail for something I didn't do, rather than all the things I've done.

"Dammit. Okay, let's split up. All we gotta do is find one."

Shayna Zimmerman

Who are these people? Why are they doing this? Whatever it is they want, how can I convince them that I don't have it?

I'm squatting under a backyard deck—I'm hoping it's the Waltham's deck, but it's so dark, I'm pretty sure it's a neighbor's house, and I don't even care if they have a dog and I get bit, because, God, at least the dog might scare away The Men.

God, I'm sorry that I only talk to you when I'm in trouble.

A few feet away there's a pond with a fountain, which makes it so that I can't hear what's happening on the grass outside (are there people out there? I can barely see anything). Not that I would be able to hear them anyway, with my breath stuttering and my heart bouncing around my ribcage like a loose animal.

When we were in third grade, and the teachers wanted us to be quiet, they just turned off the lights in the room, and everyone would put their heads down on the table, and go silent (even loud-mouths like Jen who couldn't keep her mouth shut if you paid her). But once in a while some poor kid would have the hiccups, and the more he tried to swallow them down, the louder they came out.

God, I promise not to be vain. I promise to stop making myself throw up. I promise to be nice to the ugly girls. I promise to get good grades in high school.

Was that a footstep on the deck? Is someone walking above my head?

It's actually more like a scurry—a squirrel or chipmunk, I bet. Why am I crouching under a stranger's deck in the middle of the night? Why am I surrounded by animals?

Emma Waltham

I have to run. I don't care. There is an obligation to my body deeper than what I feel towards those girls. I imagine scenarios where I have to bargain with their lives. "You can take the pretty one, and, if you want, the other two as well. But leave me and my sister alone. We weren't even supposed to leave the house tonight. We told them to stay inside." For a moment, I actually convince myself that they deserve to be hunted.

I'm five backyards away, and I can see my house in the distance. There's only one fence between me and home. But my feet won't move. I'm stuck half-buried in a sycamore, just another tree among the trees. A tree, I notice, is more alive than I've ever really realized. I realize, too, that standing around like this is what trees do all day.

The rule against walking on the neighbors' grass prevents me from making the first step. I'm poised, like an olympic runner, against the property line.

Go! Run! Do it! Don't think so hard!

I cover the first lawn in a few strides. The second lawn is full of rabbit holes, and there is a garden, and a rabbit hutch; I stamp out the budding animal and vegetable life without conscience. My foot gets snagged in a hole, and I stumble, but go on. The next lawn is the one with the fence; I roll underneath the lowest beam and get up to my feet in one motion. I think about the advice from physical education class. Run through the pain. I hurdle another patch of garden.

The grass is wet. I lost a shoe. But still, I hobble on, not caring where the shoe fell, or what happened to it, or how much it cost.

Angell Ramon

"Girls, hey. Hey, girls." I'm doing a shout-whisper, the kind you might use to call in your cat. If I find any of them, I don't know what I'd even say. I'm the friend of the brother of one of your friends and I just wanted to scare the shit out of you, did it work?

Hell, they're probably enjoying it. We used to play manhunt when we were thirteen—hide and seek, all through the neighborhood— and that's pretty much what we're doing now. If they knew they were playing, they'd be having the time of their lives, and might even let themselves be found.

Hey, if I ran into Dierdre, that would be sweet. How many times in your life does a guy run into a hot girl in her pajamas at her most vulnerable moment? Not that I'd have the slightest clue how to exploit the situation.

Not that Carla wouldn't kill me dead if she found out. But it's the makings of a porno movie plot is all I'm saying.

Every once in a while I see a shape moving in the distance, but my eyes aren't quite adjusted to the total darkness. I've gone hunting with my uncles before, but not like this, not when it's night out and the animal is just as smart as you are. It makes me think how instinctual everyone really is, how guided by needs.

My dad was a war hero, stoic as hell. My only memories of him are of the senses. His almost-metallic smell, the single vein that bulged out on his forehead, his slight lisp when his crazy lips would finally split and he'd say some crazy words.

And I remember, once, being at the dollar store where he was gonna buy me some junk to play with, and the owner of the store kept following us around. We'd turn a corner, he'd find a reason to stack the shelves in whatever aisle we were in. And he wasn't some hippy either—not one of those guys my dad complained about all the time for how ungrateful they were towards military men like he was. That owner was just a regular guy, like my dad.

Louisiana Frick

I scan the street, right-left, left-right, taking in every detail, memorizing all the site markers of this suburban battleground. I'm crouching behind a cord of firewood, peeking out. In a moment of boldness, I think about making a dash for the guys' car. Maybe the keys are left in the ignition? Maybe that's the last place they'd look? Instead, I pick up one of the few logs that fits easily into the grip of my left hand.

Left-handedness, my dad told me, used to be associated with the wicked. The word "sinister" comes from the Latin sinistre, meaning "left handed." It was one of the tests they used to determine who was a witch. When I asked my mother about this, she scoffed at my dad's explanation, and said that really all left-handedness meant was that I was "right-brained," which meant I was a "creative thinker."

Now I think my dad must be right. I'm dying for an opportunity to make use of this club. Does that make me wicked? And which would you rather be: wicked-witch material, or some old "creative thinker"?

I see Dierdre and Jen in the woodsy area not too far away. I sprint in their direction, scaring the hell out of them when I show up out of no where, panting, weapon in hand.

"Where's Emma?" Dierdre asks me, and I shrug. Strange, but I want Dierdre to comment on my safety. I want her to be thankful that I'm safe.

"What are you doing with that stick?" Jen says.

"What are you doing with that face?" I say.

"Shut up," Dierdre says, "please."

But...I want to say, she's the loud one. But at this point, saying anything at all would prove the lie.

This is just like Lou. This is just like Arizona. Her running off like that. Me worried sick, feeling like it's my fault that she's no where to be found.

I bet she knows what's going on. I bet she saw Angell's car and figured it out by now. I bet she's doing this to freak us out. Honestly, I wouldn't put it past her. But I would also bet that, given the chance, she would probably stay hidden, and never let herself be found.

By now, I'm just walking down the middle of the street, in the open, balancing on the thin white line that divides the imaginary traffic, hoping Lou finds me, and comes out and says something. "Hey, Lou!" I shout.

Let the bedroom lights click on in the house across the street. I've got nothing to hide.

Dierdre Waltham

Jen and Lou tag along behind me a few paces. Jen paws my arm.

"Do you see anything, Dierdre?" she practically yells. I hate the way she says my name: "Dair-dra."

What a lousy team we three make. Jen, who can't hold it in for five minutes, and Lou, who seems like she's actually enjoying being hunted by a bunch of psychos.

"Hey!" This voice comes from the other sidewalk, where under the streetlight I can see a figure covered by a shadow that is already angling toward us. And I swear it sounds like he's shouting, "Hey, Lou." But, after a moment's thought, I fill in the blanks, and figure out that he really said, "hey, you."

"Run!" I shout to the girls, and they do as told.

The guy starts running after us, shouting something I can't even hear over the whistling of air, splitting in front of me as I run. Which confirms two things: one, the guys in the car really are after us, and two, I should really try out for track next year.

I'm the first one home, but the door is locked. Just who are they trying to keep out, anyway? I lead the girls into the garage, where we take a side door into the house. With fumbling hands, I manage to lock it down and flip the floodlights on. The inside lights are off, and I'm looking out the window, thin-eyed and ready.

Jen Aldiss

In the darkness, Dierdre keeps saying, "Where's Emma?" and Lou and I keep saying, "I dunno." The thing that really gets to her, though, is that it doesn't seem to bother Lou very much. She repeats herself, "Where is she?"

"I don't know," says Lou.

"Who were those guys?" I asked, trying to think of something to distract Dierdre, so that our group elder doesn't go nutty. "Do you think maybe they were cops?"

Dierdre narrows her eyes at me. "It's not illegal to be outside at night," she says, "but it is illegal to drive up on the sidewalk and almost run over a bunch of people. Those guys aren't cops, they're criminals, and they were after us."

That didn't work. I have to watch my mouth sometimes. I turn to Lou.

"Lou?" I ask. "How did you get back home, when you were out there in the desert? With the snakes?"

She looks surprised. She thought I forgot, I guess.

"It's funny, but as soon as I came to terms with the fact that I was totally lost and probably was going to get bit by a snake, I calmed down, and just followed my natural compass," she says.

"What? Your 'natural compass'?" I say.

"Yeah," she says, "it was really odd. It all looked the same to me out there, with no site markers or anything, and I had no idea how to read the position of the stars or the moon or whatever, so I just picked a direction and started walking, and it brought me right home."

"Wow," I said. "You got lucky."

At that moment, Dierdre gasps. "Here comes Emma," she says, "with Shayna."

The digital clock reads 2:33 when Dierdre shakes my shoulder, and my eyelids split and, a second or two later, glue back together again. At 2:41 the lights turn on and the room is filled with lights, bodies, voices. "We were chased!"; "They're still out there!"; "We should call the police!"; "I think one of them had a gun!"; "Are all the doors locked?"; "I will never go outside again!"

Dierdre says, "Mom, get up. This is serious." But isn't everything serious these days with these girls? Aren't their lives always the center of an ongoing drama that, like daytime television, one-ups itself every episode, escalating into intricacies of plot rivaling a 13-year old version of the absurdist theater, and always having to do with boys?

I try to listen to them, to tune into their wavelength, but only static comes through, white noise at full volume, especially the curly-red-haired one who talks as though she has a right—a right!—to be listened to. And what are they talking about? I can't muster enough sympathy, I can't even fake it enough, to find out.

Dierdre is holding Emma, who is crying; Morty has taken Lou off into a corner, trying to get the facts about "the incident" (since Lou seems to be the only one with her head screwed onto her shoulders); and the other three are talking manically, hyper-linguistically, like some advanced species that can communicate at the speed of thought (but have yet to find a species that can understand them).

And I'm wondering, since they have already grouped-off now— since they seem to be settling whatever-it-is that came between them by talking (though always, of course, in a frantic, exaggerated way) and no one is bleeding or broken-boned, and they are too young to crash the car or get pregnant—if I could slip off back to bed and let their voices become the backdrop to whatever dream I was having before being shoved awake into the shared world. And as I consider the impossibility of ever returning to an old dream the way you might go back to visit an old home, Dierdre looks up from kissing Emma's head and says, "Mom, maybe you should drive Emma's friends home?"

Can you imagine? Could I have imagined, at thirteen years old, that someday I would be driving around in the middle of the night, taking directions from girls who swear they know where their houses are in the daytime, explaining to every set of parents along the way that something (but what?) scared their daughters out of their wits and sent them home in tears at 3 a.m.—daughters who are just like the girls I once knew?

DEATH OF AN IRONIST

Kenneth Frick

"Dead is the new alive," Ken said to Fran, his maybe girlfriend, over the phone. "I swear, if I have to watch any more sexy-young-American-girl-battles-the-undead shows, I'm gonna have to un-kill somebody."

"Why not just un-watch it?" she asked.

"It's un-turn-offable," he said.

"Okay. Understood."

Ken cradled the receiver between his cheek and shoulder, while he flipped the channels on the remote. He settled on a show called *Robot War!*

"Oh god, *Robot War!* is on," Ken announced.

Fran scoffed. "That's, like, pornography for engineers. How can you watch it?"

"How can you not watch it?" Ken said. "And you like pornography, by the way."

"Only the seventies stuff," Fran said, "when it was all about the hair."

There was a brief silence on both ends, which Fran hastened to fill. "I got a tattoo."

"Oh yeah? Congratulations," said Ken. He shifted in the bed, and the sheets crinkled. A slight tug on the phone cord answered with a ding that sounded to him like a gameshow buzzer.

"Why are hospitals, like, the last place in the world to use rotary phones?" he asked.

"I don't get it," Fran said.

"Nothing. Rotary phones are just funny, you know. Even out of context, a rotary phone is funny…It's like adult braces. You can't not laugh," he explained.

"Oh yeah," Fran said.

Ken looked at the remote control in his hand. Two buttons, TV and nurse. He wondered what would happen if the graphics on the buttons were worn down, so you couldn't tell which is which—some poor guy would be having a heart attack and, when he clicks for help, he gets *The Home Shopping Network*.

"So what time are you scheduled to go in?" Fran asked.

"About ten minutes ago," Ken answered. "Make that eleven minutes and twenty-nine seconds…Thirty. Thirty-one. Thirty-two. Thirty-three." Fran counted along.

"Oh, my nephew started counting the other day," Ken said. "My mom was taking him for the afternoon, and Peter starts counting, and my mom goes crazy, clapping and whooing and shit. I'm like, 'Woah, Mom, when have you ever whooed before? Maybe if you whooed at me when I learned to count, I'd be some kind of brainiac by now'."

"Shut. Up. You're too smart as it is," Fran said, using a schoolmarm voice, "You just don't apply yourself."

"Hold on, I think I'm going into the O.R. soon," Ken said, with a slight shake in his voice.

"Steal one of those robes that expose your ass for me, okay?" Fran said.

"Sure thing, sugar."

When Ken put down the receiver, Dr. Lee was standing beside him with his hands folded. "Sounds like you've got a nice girl," the doctor said, smiling.

"Yeah, she's quote nice endquote," Ken said.

"So, Ken, are you feeling any pain at the moment?" Dr. Lee asked.

Ken said, "Uh…does a constant burning feeling in my gut count?"

"On a scale of one to ten, how would you rate your pain?" said Dr. Lee.

"Oh no," Ken said, his voice sinking to bass clef, "you're not giving me the face chart test, are you? I hate the face chart."

"Think of one as mild discomfort, and ten as the most intense pain you've ever felt."

"I'm always feeling mild discomfort…Okay, let me see the face chart." Ken said.

Dr. Lee stepped out of the way, so Ken could get a clear shot at the graphic, which coded simple facial expressions into numbers.

"Well, I'm definitely a frowny face, so…seven, I guess."

Dr. Lee wrote down on his clipboard what Ken assumed was the numeral seven. "Okay, lay back now. We're just going to check your abdomen. Lift your shirt."

Ken raised his shirt, reclined, and Dr. Lee applied pressure to his stomach with his fingers. "Does that hurt?"

He shook his head. When Dr. Lee applied pressure to the other side, Ken laughed.

"Does it tickle?"

"No, no, nothing. I was just thinking of this one Simpsons episode, where Homer is at the Doctor's office..." Ken started to say.

Dr. Lee smiled indulgently, showing the wrinkles around his epicanthic eyes. "You can pull your shirt back down," he said. A man with green scrubs and a mustache walked in, and nodded to Dr. Lee. "This is Roger; he'll bring you down to the operating room."

On the walk down to the O.R., Ken noticed that the steps of the doctors in their white robes, and the nurses with their green aprons, clicked loudly on the tile, while his own steps were padded with traction socks, noiseless, no matter how hard he landed on his feet. Roger opened the double doors and guided him inside. The room had a high ceiling, and two air vents.

His body on the table now, Ken kept thinking of the game *Operation,* where kids pick out plastic organs, with tweezers, from the body of a man with male-pattern baldness and a flashing red nose. No, what he was thinking about was the TV commercial for the game, and the little blonde girl with the hairband that he used to have a crush on. *I can't believe that I remember being eight and having a crush on a ten-year old girl,* he thought, *but back then she was an older woman.* Ken, to his considerable discomfort, remembered afternoons playing doctor with his neighbor Cleo, the subtle eroticism of bodies under examination, the tantalizing mystery of unexplored regions.

The doors swung open again, and a spectacled doctor with short curly hair, even on his hands, began setting up his equipment.

"I'm Doctor Stein, the anesthesiologist, and, uh..." he looked down at his chart. "It says here you want the full treatment today?"

"Yes," Ken confirmed. "Make me numb. The less I know about it the better. Just put me to sleep. Come to think of it, don't wake me up until flannel is back in style."

"Have you ever had nitrous before?" Dr. Stein asked.

"Oh yeah. Me and nitrous go way back...we met in high school."

"All right, but just to remind you, it feels funny when you go under, so don't panic, okay?" Dr. Stein held the mask out to Ken, and he took it in his hands. "Hold that over your mouth and nose, while I plug you in here…"

As soon as Ken inhaled the sweet-burning gas, his body tensed and released. The suddenness of the loss of consciousness felt surprisingly like death, and despite the doctor's recent warnings, his pulse quickened. His mind raced through a thousand scenarios, all of them ending in his demise. In one of them, his body was a bridge, and a parade of cartoon characters was crossing over his back to the world of the flesh; his body broke apart into pieces, leaving the river strewn with puppets, dwarves, and superheroes.

In another, he was in an infomercial for fitness equipment; the machine would not stop, and an aging B-list actress goaded him on with cries of, "Do you feel the burn?" Knowing that this should be funny, he tried to laugh, but could not. The pain in his legs was too strong to exorcise.

Realizing suddenly that he should be feeling no pain, that he should be numb, he was transported to a hospital room, not unlike the one he had just left, his body wasting at the speed of time-lapse photography. A wilting flower. Mold growing on a peach. A city with the sun speeding through the sky. His life flashing before his eyes? It all seemed so trivial, and contrived, as though it were cobbled together by corporate profiteers, approved by a focus group, and none of it living up to the weightiness of death that he'd been promised. Is this mortal life? He wondered. This constant distraction from itself?

A laugh-track answered him. He was standing on a stage, with the kind of light that reveals everything, conceals shadow, erases every blemish on the face with a uniform whiteness. He stepped out into the center. He was a sitcom star, making an unexpected appearance from stage right, delivering a well-timed punch-line, standing in poses of incredulity. His arms awkwardly turned out to the sides, with his palms up, as though begging for change.

Made in Taiwan

Cam Trung

Birds mix in the courtyard behind the restaurant, chatting over animal remains. Bao shoos them away, flapping his apron back and forth like the wing of a larger bird. They scatter and return.

"The fucking fan is broken," Bao says to Khanh, standing halfway inside the kitchen. Khanh's bald pate is broken up by lines of sweat.

"Ya," he says, squeezing pastry dough between his thumbs and forefingers. "No good."

Bao squeezes through to where I stand, hunching over a running tub of suds with plastic gloves on. "The fucking fan is broken," he says.

So I shuck off the gloves and walk outside to the dumpster. Our large fan hasn't spun since this morning. I unlatch the cage front, and let it hang by its hinges. Inside, the blades of the fan are gummy with years of dust, droppings, and mold. I feel the thickness of the grime with my fingers—I just have to. I've never touched anything so ugly; not even drunk. With its propeller exposed, I think, if the motor fired up, I'd die in filth.

I turn on the hose and hold the nozzle, getting into appropriate spraying stance. I fire a concentrated blast of water into the mesh of steel, then the dumpster. When I let go, and the virile stream of the hose cuts off into a trickle, you can hear dripping all around, from the fan to the wall, the wall to the floor, and from floor to the drain. No birds.

I close the cage, click the fan on; it sputters with life, and blows my hair into a raven's wing.

The tables here are sandwiches of wood, white cloth, and glass. I'm in a mahogany booth puffing on my last Lucky Strike, staring between the fingers of a ceramic hand. Chann, a Cambodian refugee kid, ex-Khmer, made hundreds of these mannequin hands for specialty shops to use for modeling gloves and rings. He made all of them by hand, and they're all molded after his own long, articulate fingers. I liked them so much I bought one for no particular reason.

Hung walks in even thinner and darker than I remember him. I wave him over, and he slides into the seat opposite me in the booth. "Look at you: Mr. American," he says.

"You look like a Malay," I say.

He smiles like a sneer. "I've been taking my bike in the sun," he says, by way of explanation. "What's this thing for?" he adds, noticing the hand.

"It's not for anything," I say. "Just to look at."

"Waste of time," he says.

"I'd offer you a cigarette…" I say, showing him the empty box. He fans the air like he can't stand the smell all of a sudden. I tap out the ash from the tip of the cig and insert it between the middle and forefinger of the ceramic hand, where it raises a steady line of thin smoke. Hung is here to offer me a job where I don't have to handle moldy birdshit, so I figure I owe it to him not to blow smoke in his face. Still, it was his idea to meet at the restaurant where I work. He can't expect me to douse my last cigarette.

"You ready to order?" asks Jen, our waitress.

"Could we have some menus, actually?" I ask.

"Sure," she says, and scams us a couple of laminated sheets marked "luncheon specials."

Hung shakes his head. "You work here, and don't know what to order? Bad sign."

"I'm eating here, right?" I check myself. "Hey, don't you want a menu?"

As if to prove his point, Hung signals Bao over and orders in rapid-fire Vietnamese. Meanwhile, Jen returns and stands behind Bao, forming a queue.

"I'd like the Pho special," I say, leaning back to address the second-in-line.

Hung scoffs. "It's not *Fo*, it's *Fuh*." The first word he pronounces with an exaggerated F, and the second he pronounces with a lingering bass U.

"Well, I hope you're hungry," I say. "The catfish is fresh—a ten pounder." Khanh takes his time cooking up the Ca Kho To, which wins us a few complaints from walk-in customers now and then, but Hung and I don't expect our food fast.

"You catch it yourself or something?" Hung asks.

"Right out of the canal," I say with a laugh.

"The only fish you'll catch in there are rats," he says.

I hear "rats" and I almost forget who I'm talking to; I almost go defensive, pointing out that in Vietnam they eat field rats, not filthy sewer rats like they have here. Tastes better than cow.

"That explains the feet;" I say, "you know, it had whiskers, so I thought it was catfish."

"Ratfish," he says, and we laugh as though we're still students together.

Right then, I'm tempted to talk about the bird-shit incident earlier today, to test him, maybe, but I quickly remember who is here to test who.

"So why'd you want to meet here, eh?" I ask.

"Do you know any other places in Providence?" he counters.

"There's always Thai," I say, just to get a reaction.

"Ah, you're such a hamburger," he says, and the subject drops. I can only guess at his reasons. Eating in the same restaurant that you work proves you've got a stomach. Otherwise who knows what kinds of plastic tubes they might use to funnel food inside you. You could be made in Taiwan. You could be a McDonald's Playland.

"Why is there soy sauce on these tables? Who's gonna put soy sauce on Vietnamese food?"

"Our customers don't like fish sauce." I feel like I should apologize for the condiments.

"Who asked your customers?" he says, exasperated.

"You run a business," I say, "Isn't the customer always right?"

"Not real estate customers," he puts in.

Hung stares out the window, at the Hope St. traffic, and I know what he's thinking: a real place would have set up a cart in an alley rather than pander to tourists; a real owner would hire his loudmouth cousin to call out to passersby on the street and lure them in.

He puts his reading glasses on, and thumbs through a pile of papers on a clipboard.

"So why do you want to work in real estate?" he asks.

I shift in my seat, calibrating my body to the new mood in the room. "I'm ready to be serious, to handle more responsibility, make more money—"

"Well," he cuts in, "that depends on you. You get paid for selling houses."

"Yeah," I say, pausing, "and I think I'd be good at it."

"How do you know, working here all the time?" he asks, and it's a surprisingly good question. Why the hell would I be good at selling houses?

I hesitate. "I let the customers make their own decisions, and they respect that," I wind up saying, "I accommodate their needs, but I don't push them to buy things they don't want."

Hung stops scribbling on his pad. "What do you mean, don't push? That's what selling is. How can you sell houses if you don't push for them to buy?"

"Okay, okay," I say, "let me explain. I think, if the customer is coming to me, okay, they are already looking to buy a house. And when it comes to houses…like food, too…people know what they like, but they don't know how to find it—so my job is to help them find what they are looking for, no?"

"No," says Hung, and scribbles on his pad again. Then, "What was the worst job you ever had?"

This time I answer without hesitation. "Mall security."

"Why? So many thieves?" he asks.

"No. My whole job was waiting. The whole time I worked there I'd just be waiting; watching, waiting for someone to do something wrong."

As he eats, Hung watches—how well my hands manipulate the chopsticks, if I use the wrong sauce on the wrong dishes, and when it comes to the bottom of the soup bowl, whether I bring it up to my lips and slurp, or finish it spoonful by spoonful, in the Western way.

Hung's eyes linger on Jen as she waves at me, walking from the booth to the kitchen. "You like that?" he asks me, in Vietnamese.

I understand just enough to get his insinuations. "The gio is a little weak, but the pho is good," I say, pretending not to notice. I'm no gentleman, but when it comes to Jen, I get enough heat from Bao and Khanh just for chatting her up between shifts.

"Fuh," Hung corrects me, low and long on the U again.

Between bites, I pick up the ceramic hand and hold it up to my mouth to smoke from it.

"This place could use some work," Hung says, prodding the walls gingerly as though he expected them to crumble.

At that point, I'm about at the end of my tether. "Are you here to offer me a job, or are you here to buy the building?"

"Me? I'm always thinking of buying and selling buildings, which is why I work in real estate. What do you want to do, eh? Serve soy sauce with coca-cola? Flirt with white waitresses who got the yellow fever?"

"You're disgusting," I say, with a grimace.

"What? You saying you don't flirt with the white waitress?" he asks, disbelieving.

"No. I mean…soy sauce with coca-cola? That's disgusting. Can't you see I'm eating?"

"Okay," he says, after the plates are cleared, "you come work for me. Start next week."

"Good," I answer, confident now that there was nothing I could have done so wrong that he would have hired someone else.

Hung calls Jen over and pays in cash without looking at the bill.

Pointing to my hand sculpture, he says, "Don't keep stuff like that in your office, okay? It will make customers think you are weird."

"But this is a hand-made hand," I say, "it's a conversation starter."

"No, it's not. That stuff is Made in Taiwan, okay?" Hung says, getting up from the booth, and putting his papers back into his briefcase. "Okay?"

"Okay," I say, not knowing what it is I'm saying "okay" to.

Hung rushes out, the bill having been paid, and the interview concluded.

My last cigarette is burning down. With a Lucky Strike, you don't know which end to smoke from, or when the smoke is over.

Jen takes a seat at the booth after the lunch rush. She reaches over, and I hand her the last centimeter of cigarette, and she puffs delicately, like a Frenchwoman, as though she's kissing smoke, and hands it back.

"So, you're gonna sell houses now, huh?" she says.

I shrug. "Until something better comes along," I say.

Jen thumbs the napkins, unconsciously counting how many are left in the dispenser.

"Well, don't let him get to you," she says, "he doesn't know me."

"Apparently, neither do I," I say, "You speak Vietnamese?"

"Better than you," she says, pinching my cheek like an affectionate Aunt. And I can either act like I'm offended, or douse the cig, and pinch her back.

Body Art

Jerry McGowan

When I bought the business back in '81, Darren was a part of the package. I remember telling Evan, the old owner, that I wanted to bring in my own guy, and he said, Great, as long as I kept Darren around too. I figured him for a charity case, someone Evan had "taken in" during his Al Anon period, and reformed with the promise of a steady job. The only other Haitians I knew were hustlers, and I was none too pleased to have one manage the place by himself three days a week.

But Darren turned out different from what I expected. He was a real talent, and straight as a book edge. Too straight for a tattoo man, maybe. But as long as he could etch from a pattern, and the customers left happy, eventually I counted myself lucky to be getting such a loyal hand in the bargain.

"So how did you and Evan meet up?" I asked him, just sitting around on a slow day.

"I first come to Providence a long time ago. I do street portraits. I introduce him his wife," Darren replied, shrugging his shoulders, as though it were a familiar story.

"Like, what? You're doing drawings out there on the canal, and Evan comes up to you and asks you to hook him up?"

Darren shakes his head. "I do two portraits same time. I give wrong one to each of them, tied with…ribbon. Later, when they look at picture, they see each other. They curious. So they come back next day. I not there, but they see each other."

"C'mon. You did it on purpose?" I asked.

Darren shrugged his shoulders again.

"Well, you better not pull that shit in here. I don't want people getting the wrong tattoos." I looked out at the foot traffic from the shop window. I could almost feel the money pissing out of that place into the sewer.

Darren could be a sonovabitch. He never drank, but he had a

seasonal barometer that, in the summer, made him a real jackal. The guy never stopped laughing from June to September. I'd cuss him out, and hurl as many racial slurs as only an Outlaw can, and Darren would bust out laughing even harder, and look at me and call me howdy doody.

"You don't like white folks much, do you, Darren?" I asked him once.

"Of course I like white folks," he said. "They make best canvasses. I try to draw pink rose on a black ass, and it looks like bruise." He convulsed with laughter, and held his hand in front of his mouth, to stop the spittle.

"I don't get you, Darren," I said.

"Hey, how come people always wanna tattoo on they ass?" Darren said, and after that he wouldn't stop laughing till we closed and went home.

It was the late nineties, and Darren and me had been in business some eighteen years. We made enough to keep us afloat, but we never had a big boom, the way other industries had. You could say I was disappointed at our progress. We hadn't expanded beyond the two of us. And Darren put in so many hours, I guess I never really felt the need. But still, when I'd check the books, it seemed a sorry return for almost two decades of investment.

In the latest of a series of efforts to go digital, I got a security cam that could be hooked up to the computer. Just as urban crime began to go down, the price of security went down too, so we finally bought in just as the neighborhood gangs were calling it quits. But what I learned from watching Darren on the security cam surprised me about as much as any robbery would've.

The first one was a college girl who spent like an hour looking at the laminated swatches in the booklet, before ultimately deciding on a Maori fetish that she wanted etched on her left shoulder. Darren frowned, and said that maybe since she was so young she should get something a little less pagan. Then he showed her all the Jesus stuff we have, and said that if she wanted a tattoo, she should get something she'd never regret. She declined, and said that she really did want the Maori fetish, and they went back and forth arguing

74

until Darren finally gave up, and started prepping her for the idol he was about to bestow on her. But I stood there for a while afterwards, tipping on my heels.

The next one was a big guy who had a number of tattoos already, and it seemed like he'd been in there before.

"Changed your mind, Howie?" Darren asked.

"Naw, I'm gonna go with the bitch on the bike with the big titties," he said.

"Suit yourself," said Darren.

And it went on, and some of the customers would walk out on him, and some of them would cave in and get a baby in a manger, or a fish arrow, and some of them would talk and talk to him like Darren was somebody important. And he gave away some free of charge. There it was, our own "Voodoo Tattoos,"—the name I'd given the place because Darren was Haitian—and here he was proselytizing the most un-Voodoo kind of shit I ever heard. There you had it, the church of Darren, a beggar's business, funded right out of my own pocket. I almost snapped.

Next day, I showed up early and waited for Darren to make his appearance. When he did, he came through the jangling door, and a look passed between us that left no misunderstandings.

"Why didn't you tell me, that's all I'm wondering," I said. I'd had all night to simmer, and by morning I knew that I wasn't going to fire him. For better or worse, our destinies were mixed, and I was getting too old to cope with any big changes. I certainly didn't want some new kid from the art school walking around like he ran the place.

"I help people," he said, with rare gravity.

"Aw, bullshit," I said. "You used me, Darren. If you cared so much about saving souls, why didn't you ever pull that shit with me? What, the light of the Lord don't shine on old Jerry? Or did you think I'd shut down your little operation here if I knew what you were up to?"

"You angry I give people faith while work for you? Or you angry I not give you faith?" he said.

"We don't sell faith here, man. This here is Voodoo Tattoos. We sell body art."

"Then I am an artist, and I know what is best."

75

So now I deal with his pious bullshit every goddamn day. But, though he still pisses me off no end, and he cracks jokes at me all summer, and we argue pedestrian theology when nobody's around and the clock is running on both of our paychecks, Darren and I manage to share the business without it coming down to muskets; and I've got to thinking recently that this is just the existence for an old man who people never liked much, and who never much liked people either.

THE MANHATTAN PROJECT

Red Manhattan

DJ's on line one. The light on the phone flashes green. Bass line pumps through the soundboard and plaster. I pick up, but I can't hear shit except, "stuck…"

Zero better not be making excuses. "Put him on speaker."

Click.

"…a show out in Foxwoods last night. It rained. The van's stuck in the mud. Can't you get Cid to cover?" Zero says, through the cracked speaker.

"Take a taxi. We'll use the house equipment. Hurry your ass up here," I say.

"Naw, naw. I gotta wait for triple-A," Zero says.

"What the fuck? Triple-A?! Leave the keys with a roadie for Chrissakes! Get your ass up to Providence or I'm sending an escort." I plug the speaker button with my thumb, sending his voice into oblivion. I have a thing for sudden endings.

Bronte sits there in a metal chair, waiting for marching orders.

"Zero's got a new name," I say. Pause for the punchline. "DJ Triple-A."

The way he laughs is to shake his head.

"Triple-A," I repeat to myself. "I swear if I find out that punk was at the blackjack table all morning, I'll cut him off at the knees."

"At the balls," he says, and I can't hold back a wince.

~

Bronte and I talk tough but we don't mean nothing by it. As long as our records are straight, so are we. We keep each other in business. I mean, Bronte's the one who got me in here in the first place.

It's almost nine. So I have him go look for Zero, because Bronte's the best escort I have. I say escort, maybe you think hooker. But Bronte's business is security. I say security, maybe you think flunky, meathead. But good security is royalty in the Rhode Island club circuit. These guys run the show. I'm just there to keep it respectable.

"You sure?" he says. "You cool for a while?"

"DJ hits the floor at midnight. Bring 'im back by then," I say.

"You sure?" he says, one more time. I nod. "All right. Sit tight. If I'm not back by midnight, find another DJ, all right?"

"Yeah, sure. But I want to get Zero to DJ tonight. Otherwise all the scenesters will go south."

I watch him shrink in the hallway through the glass door. I roll my chair to the balcony side, and look out onto the pits. The whole place is decorated with pipes, TNT candles, and mushroom clouds. Bodies are dancing but everyone's waiting for the real shit to start.

Zero's on the bill, but I'm trying to track down Cid just in case. After about an hour I get his boyfriend on the phone, tells me his man is down in Baltimore. I catch myself scratching at a scab. I swear, if I didn't own the club, I'd jump ship. One down night can end a place. The ghosts'll find some other hood to haunt.

Suddenly there's this voice, says, "What stinks?" Up in front of me now there's a face I almost don't recognize because of a straight-across eighties mustache. Then when I figure out who it is, I start picking my scab again.

"Don't you know the smell of your own ass?" I say, looking down at the papers in front me as if they mean something.

"Red! What gives, man?" He's standing there with his arms open, like a statue of Atlas waiting for the globe to fall in.

"Nothing. I'm busy right now. I have a lot on my mind. I'm a working man." I still won't look at him.

"What am I, a deadbeat?" he says. I snort in spite of my cool. We were runaways together.

"Look. Just tell me what you want, Flip." I look him in the eyes now, steady as a hypnotist.

"Hey, I'm fine. I didn't come out here because I wanted something from you. You're the one who looks like he's got the Sword of Damocles over his head." He takes a seat like I'd invited him in.

"Nice. Where'd you get that shit? Sword of Damocles?" I need something to do with my hands. I open the drawer and take out a pack of Lucky Strikes.

"Oh, I go back to the classics now and then. Man-o-War, Iron Maiden, you know." He watches me light up with something like toleration. "Seriously. What's your trouble?"

I have a way of looking that makes it seem like I'm weighing a man's sincerity, like I can look into his head; but really I'm just waiting for him to talk first.

"Let's grab a drink," he says. "Whatever it is, it's nothing a coupla drinks won't cure." He goes to pick me up by the shoulder like it's an intervention.

"Wait." I stop him. It probably shows in my eyes, "You ever spin?"

He leaves me in suspense for a few seconds. "Nope. C'mon."

Flip was supposed to be an abortion. But his Mama got pulled aside and "justified" by Christians on the sidewalk of the clinic, and so she promised to let fate decide instead. She called him Coinflip, because that's the only reason he made it out alive. The thing is, though, that Flip is always telling you about it, to show you how little dying means to him.

"You see, a guy like me expects to get shit on because I've been shit on all my life. Half a chance I wouldn't even have been born. Now you, Red, you take everything so hard." We're sitting at a table in a crowded jazz bar, and Flip philosophizes at me while I smoke.

"Is that right?" I say, just humoring him.

"Yup. That's what happens when you get too lucky in life. You forget that it's all just Maya."

"Maya?" I say.

"That's right. The veil of the world. Everything that happens, all this bullshit around you, is just Maya, masking the true sight from you."

I stare at him for what I think is a long time. Flip is always showing up and talking crazy, but this was something else. I pull out a ten-spot and slap it on the table. "Go get us some drinks, you beatnik."

He kicks back his chair and fades into the mess of bodies. For a second it's only me and a cloud of smoke.

Flip comes back to the table with something orange, like it should have an umbrella in it.

"Whatsis?" I ask him. I'm handling it like nuclear waste.

"Supernova. House special." He has a stupid grin and a mustache to top it off. "Plus I added something good to it."

I shrug and take a dram. It stings the lips. "Fug," I say, putting it down on the table as far from me as I can reach. He's laughing. Flip has that gleam of mischief that you think of toddlers as having, or Nascar racers.

"Good, huh?" He chugs it quick. "That's a supernova."

"That's a Chevy Nova...or somethin'. Shit is foul." I'm still hacking on the first sip. But five minutes later my throat is so dry with menthol I'm reaching for the stuff.

~

"Let's say time is a highway and you're a truck driver," Flip starts. My head isn't totally clear, but I think all I did was ask him the time. "It's past midnight and there's no exit for fifteen miles or more— until you reach your where yer goin', in fact."

"It's past midnight?" I ask him, startling myself upright. We're sitting on a city bench and the moon's out and the wind's circling the trees—making 'em dance.

"No, no. I'm talking metaphorically here," he says.

"Oh," I say. "Go on."

"All right. So you're drivin' and you're drivin' and you're drivin', and you're getting sleepy, and the whole time you're thinking, God, I hope I don't get into an accident, I hope I don't get pulled over, I hope I make it on time and none of the stock is damaged, right?" He looks to me for approval.

"Yeah, I guess. I dunno. I'm not a truck driver," I say, dodgy.

"Yes you are. In this scenario you are," he says back. "But the point is, you're out there cruisin', just in the world, Red, and all you're thinking about is all the shit that could happen, or will happen—

but what's happening, man, right now, is you've pulled over. Time is stopped." The pitch in his voice at this point is trembling, manic.

"How high are you?" I ask him.

He looks at me slightly confused. "Hi, how are you?" He finally says. The pores on his face deepen, and the currents of muscle in his face contract, out of synch with what looks to me like glow-in-the-dark skin. His irises flare. Supernova.

Flip just came to town for the Greater Pawtucket Mustache Contest, and he says they have a DJ there. The guy plays nothing but disco, but he can keep the room alive. And frankly by this time my standards are on the fade. I'm even contemplating footing it back to the office and hitting up one of my bar-mitzvah-grade contacts.

"You sure this guy's good?" I ask, as we walk on the street side of the curb.

"Sure I'm sure. He had the room hoppin'. I'm telling you." Flip is speaking sort of mechanically and looking down, like his mind is too busy putting one foot in front of the other to focus on much else. I look down too, trying to see what he sees, and I notice there's a rhythm to our walk, slightly off-step, and an echo that trips up the walls of the alley to God knows where.

Left to my own thoughts, I start to imagine the club in chaos, on fire, raided by feds. "I shouldn't have left the floor." I say, coming to a sudden stop. Everything around, even my own hands, seems slo-mo. Right about now, Bronte and his boys must be getting anxious back at the Project.

"C'mon, you won't be sorry," Flip says. "It's only another six blocks or so." He nudges me with an elbow, like I'm a stiff he doesn't want to touch with his hands. When I start walking again, not only time has folded, but sight too, and it's like I'm watching us from the outside, distant, like a remembered body, or a dream.

From Benefit Street, it looks like the river's on fire, sending white ash and steam all over the city. I turn toward Flip to see if he is sharing the hallucination. He doesn't seem phased, but he's got that mustache-grin I hate to look at. He catches my stare, and he turns it back on me. "You've never been to the Waterfire? How long you been underground, man?"

With his okay, I look again, and this time I see the art students with their elaborate get-ups, the kids with their cotton candy and popcorn, and the jugglers, and all the funhouse crap you get at any old festival. Under the illusion of chemistry, it only seemed sublime.

"Isn't it Atlantean?" Flip says.

I stare at him, dumbfounded again. "Where did you get all this bullshit you're talking? Is this Maya, too?"

Flip nods sagely. I am about ready to ditch him and stumble my way back to the club. But my attention is fixed on this one live mannequin in the square, a woman wearing a long white gown and a silver mask. Posing on a pedestal that reads, "Warwick Bridal Shop," she captures with her stillness something that I'm dying to put into words, but can't.

⁓

"So where's the Mustache Contest going down?" I ask Flip later, after I'm recovered.

"Oh, that's probably over by now. You could probably guess who was there by the facial hair though." He points out a few mustachioed men in the crowd.

"But what about the DJ? Flip?" I'm getting hot in the face now. "Didn't you say we were gonna go nab their DJ?"

Flip shrugs. "What can I say, man? It's like one in the morning."

"What the...you dragged me out here for nothing?" I say, and my fingers are making fists without even trying.

"Relax, Red. Let's get out of the spotlight here." He nudges me toward the pub and tries to look innocent. I'm not having it. "C'mon. We'll have another drink. We'll talk like civilized people. Then I'll be out of your hair. Promise."

I'm still standing my ground.

"Last time I saw you, you were panicked over...what was it, some sweetheart?" He's holding the door open.

⁓

I get the drinks this time, cold mugs of Guinness on tap. Though my nerves are still quivering from the supernova. And I'm sucking on another cig. Flip is taking the moment to philosophize at me some more, and his lips look like they're moving auctioneer fast. I can't follow him. My mind is slowing, and I basically don't care what he's saying.

"Stop," I say, and he quits it. "Stop bullshitting me, Flip."

Then it's like he can't help himself. "But I'm not bullshitting you, Red. Self...is an illusion. We only think we're all separate people—that...that, we're alone in the world; because that's just biology. That's just matter. But, but it's a test."

I stand up to go hit the john, just shaking my head. "Hold that thought," I say. I walk off because that's all I can do to keep my head clear. What's that cat thinking about? No opiate can do a number like that alone. It must be psychosomatic, or metaphysic, or something like that. Anyway his brain's fried. That much is clear.

I'm dry on account of the smoke and the nerves, so it only takes me a minute, and soon as I get back I see Flip scribbling in his notebook. Then when he spies me he slips it under the table like I wouldn't notice. So now I'm curious.

"What you writing there, Flip?" I ask him, casual. He shrugs. But he looks sketchy; I mean, even sketchier than usual. "No, really. What are you writing down?"

He tries to play it cool though, and he slaps it back on the table. "Just notes. I take notes on things, just in case I'll ever want to use it for an article or something."

I could slug the bastard. "You're writing about me?"

"Not about *you*. I mean, not *about* you. Just taking notes is all," he says.

I've been infiltrated. Betrayed. "You piece 'a shit. What're you tryin' to be, Hunter S. Thompson here?"

"Hold up. Stay cool, now. You're as wasted as I am," he says, making the cool-down motion with his hand, the one that looks like massaging the air.

I could kick myself. I knew the guy wrote arty little zines for local fags. "You selling me out, Flip? You gonna use me?" I'm fingering his notebook. Making him nervous. "Am I some Guido you wanna pump for a story in your fairy magazine?" I knock down the whole table, maybe cause I'm out of my head or maybe cause I need to be taken seriously. I charge out of there with a filter still smoldering on my lips.

~

The disco globe at the Manhattan Project is shaped like an a-bomb, and like the one at Hiroshima it has dirty pictures drawn on it. Like the one at Hiroshima too, it leaves shadows on the walls.

Before I even get there I know they found Zero because the tunes are rolling out like red carpet. Middle of the night and freaks are still out there waiting for an opening. Maybe just to get a reaction, I take the front door. Bronte's boys give me a cold reception, but they don't even try to keep me out of the castle.

Inside, the energy is up. Frenetic. Feels like blood is moving through me for the first time since I left. I move through the sea of dancers like an eel, dodging stray hips and elbows. As I step up toward the booth, I almost regret the nuclear theme. That's gonna get us in trouble some day.

I walk in the office, not too surprised to see both Bronte and Rory there waiting in the metal chairs, which are reserved just for guys like them. "Hey fellas," I say, and go to take the rolling chair.

"Sorry, Red," Bronte says, stopping me with his big beefy palms. "You shouldn't 'a left me to clean up your mess."

"Wait a minute. You think I've been gone on purpose? You think I jumped ship? Listen to me, man. You owe me that much, Bronte." I was too dazed to defend myself. I hardly knew what happened. I just wanted the world to slow down.

"Doesn't matter. You know there are consequences." Bronte smacks me on the cheek like it's nothing; like I'm his mutt. He's holding my shirt too, and I'm not doing shit about it either.

"All right. Fuck you, then." And that's when they really let go on me. I go limp.

~

It's the best fucking sunrise I've ever seen, with bloody light falling on everything, Van-Gogh-ing the Atlantic tide on the ports of Providence. My face is numb and blazing hot at the same time. It's hard to tell where the gauze ends and my skin begins.

I reach over and hit speaker, then say, "Flip Conner." It dials. Rings. A machine.

"Hey, uh…Flip. You're either sleepin' or you should be sleepin'. Listen, man. Forget about last night. You write your fuckin' thing. In fact, I'll even help you come up with shit for it. How were you planning on having it end? Cause I got an idea. You could have him be, like, a covert FBI guy who was just pretending to run a club so he can infiltrate the underworld, and he finally finds where all the drug lords hang out but he decides that he can't arrest them because then they'd all get out of jail in a week and he'd be on the lam the rest of his life.

"Anyway, so he sets off a bomb or something in their building, but something goes wrong and he gets hit with it too, you know, shrapnel or something…and he's put in a wheelchair for the rest of his life and all he can do is think. You know. Just sit there and fuckin' think.

"How's that sound? Good? Good."

I blot out the white noise. I don't like leaving messages.

PENNY ARTIFACTS

Abigail Gray

Right now, on the formica table where most mornings we eat our fiber cereal, there is a note from my husband that begins, *I will never be good*. For a moment, I think the hand that wrote it must belong to our son Peter, because the letters are too jagged, the lines too free, for a civil engineer turning fifty in a week. And the words are petulant, crowding the page like onlookers to a fight.

I will never be good. Every day I think that this will be the day that I become good. But it never is. And I am through waiting, it goes on.

If I pause, and picture myself in the kind of film where husbands leave notes for their wives (the kind of film John would hate), I can almost pull together the threads of his life, but then I let go, like balloon strings, and the impression falters, drifts away. He *was* a good man, I tell myself, slipping into the past tense.

How much goodness did he think I wanted? The whole thing seemed too flimsy to believe. I almost continue with the day, pour myself breakfast, put down his letter, and read the cereal boxes instead. It would be that easy. Moments of magnitude never happen, I tell myself; they are for television only.

But instead, I call his sister, who works as a croupier at Foxwoods, and who I know would be home this early.

"Hello?" she answers in a foggy voice.

"Hi, Beth. Do you know where John is?" I ask, sounding nonchalant.

"At work, probably," Beth answered.

I'm silent for a moment. In fact, I can imagine John waking up early, deciding to abandon me, writing a note, and going off to work as usual. No flight to Honolulu, no freedom drive with the speakers blasting. Just a statement of his intentions. A memo to family.

"He hasn't mentioned anything to you ever about taking a trip?" I inquire.

"No-o. Are you guys fighting?" Now Beth is awake. She used to be a social worker, so she takes an interest in others' problems.

"How can we be fighting if he isn't even here?" I say, my voice rising in pitch. "Can you think of anywhere he might go?"

"No," she says, "I can't think of anything. But if he comes by work tonight, I'll tell him to call you."

"If he shows up at Foxwoods, Beth, you call me, and I'll put a hold on our bank cards." I wind up saying. It's a pretty lousy threat. John's never been a betting man.

~

I'm six years old in a restroom stall at Camp Reddish, and my dad is waiting outside. Every now and then he knocks, asks if I'm okay, like I might need help going to the bathroom.

"I'm fine, dad," I say, "go away."

He knocks again.

"Go away!"

A moment later, I am washing my hands. The water is scalding hot. I am the best little hand-washer I know. But the liquid soap is a radioactive shade of pink and smells of ammonia, and the heat-dryers make me feel like there's a fat man breathing on my hands.

Creeped out by the hum and glow of the fluorescent light, I rush out the door, and Dad is nowhere to be found. I told him to go away, and he just went away.

Outside, it's just dark enough to see bats. There's a goose in the lake, hissing at everything that approaches, which includes me.

When I get back to the campsite, dad already has a fire going. He and my big brother Don are roasting marshmallows without me.

"Hey, Abby," he says, "I knew you'd find your way."

~

Peter walks into the kitchen with boxers and a black tee, opening up the fridge and slouching into it. "With *whom* were you just having intercourse?" he asks, in a playful, lazy-Brit accent.

"Aunt Beth," I say, turning my attention to cutting up the

potatoes on the butcher block. I need something, quick, to do with my hands.

"Well I should say you were very loud indeed in your intercourse," he says, and I feel suddenly as though he is too old to be acting this obnoxious.

I turn around abruptly, my voice as jagged as the serrated knife in my hand, "You don't have to talk like that."

"Wow," he says with a stare. "Just…wow." And he brings a couple sodas back down to the basement where he lives. At the moment, I'm not so much upset that John has left, but that he left me with Peter. *Now that our son is eighteen, does he think that he's finished?* I find that my chopping has become uselessly aggressive.

I leave the potatoes quartered, and snap up the goodbye letter from the table before going down to the basement. I go down there so seldom, all I see are the rearrangements, the absences. Wasn't there a drum set down here at one point? Why is the bed always moving from place to place, like a restless sleeper?

Peter is listening to *Sweeney Todd*, of all things.

"I'm sorry, Honey," I say. "It's just…your father wrote us a letter." I hold it up, as though he can read it from two yards away.

For a flash, a look of horror crosses his face, and I realize what kind of filling-in-the-blanks he must be doing. *No, I want to tell him, he isn't dead.* John's not that dramatic.

"Here, take a look." I hand him the letter hastily, and he scans it, uncomprehendingly. With his flannel sheets and moppet hair, he looks Disney-Channel friendly. Cute and harmless.

I can't shake that look—the same look he used to make when, fifteen years ago, he'd reach for the wrong hand in a crowd, and look up to see someone other than his mother.

"I don't get it," he says, after a while.

I open my mouth to offer an explanation, but nothing comes out.

The potatoes upstairs are beginning to turn brown, I'll bet.

―

"Men are goddamn magicians," my grandmother says, in her slow

country drawl. We are laying on a blanket in her yard. This is my respite from school and the city. I'm not quite adjusted to my new life as an Eastern urbanite—retreating to Oklahoma feels like a dark secret. But the stars out here are abundant as children in a southern family, and their nearness makes me feel like I am among them.

"Men are goddamn magicians," she says, "and I don't mean they all have disappearing acts. I mean they will always fool you and try to make it feel like awe."

What am I supposed to do, Gran, never get close to a man?

"No. Course not. Just...when you're the audience, Abby, don't applaud."

But what if *I'm the goddamn magician, I want to say, but it's too much to confess to my Presbyterian grandmother in the middle of a field in Oklahoma.*

On the drive down to Foxwoods, there's precious little distraction. In front of and behind you, there is only the striping on the road—a million yellow arrows urging you on and on and on. Everything else is tree. So much wilderness, I feel as though I could steer off the highway and become a woodland creature, briefly, suspended in the space between asphalt and pine, before the crash.

"So, Ma. What are you thinking about?" Peter asks, and I'm so proud to have a son who wants to know what his mother is thinking, that I forget whatever thoughts I just had.

"Oh, the usual, I guess," I answer. And it is now, right now, that I realize something so simple: my son will never get to know me as I was when I was his age.

"The usual," Peter says in a robot voice.

"Okay, I'm lying. I was actually having a weird fantasy," I say, committing to the truth—not out of any loyalty to principles, but out of an idle fear of seeming boring in front of my son.

"Gross," he says.

I tap Peter on his unruly head of hair. "Not *that* kind of weird fantasy. It was more like a death fantasy. I was just picturing the car going over the divider and crashing into those woods." I pointed.

The ensuing silence is made more excruciating by the endless tick-tick-tick of the Olds, which no mechanic has been able to cure. It takes a few hundred rotations of the wheel for me to realize that it's up to me—Mom—to make everything better.

"Maureen Stanton calls it Opposite Reaction Syndrome," I say. I do my best to remember the quote: "It's when the thing you least want to think or do is exactly what you think of doing: laughing at a funeral, or thrusting your hand down a garbage disposal."

"Does this happen to you a lot?" he asks, trying and failing to sound light-hearted.

More than I will ever tell.

"Well, sometimes," I say, "but I would never act on it. That's the whole point."

For example, right now I am thinking of masturbation, even though it is the last thing I would ever actually do while driving in a car, with my son riding shotgun.

"What are we going to do if we find Dad?" he asks. "Are we going to spy on him?"

Peter sounds a little too eager at the prospect.

I laugh at the absurdity of it, but I don't say no.

~

"Juliet was fourteen," Dick says, "when she banged Romeo."

"But Richard," I say, because I refuse to call him Dick. " Juliet died. They both did."

He stares away like the right words are written in the distance. "Okay, but that was before condoms were invented," he argues. "We're sixteen, man. What are we waiting for? The frickin' Age of Aquarius?"

I shrug and look coy.

"What if I were drafted tomorrow, and you never saw me again?" he said.

"Lame," I say, with a smile that I know is teasing, but can't help it, "lame lame."

"You're telling me that if I went off to war, and you didn't know whether the next time you saw me it would be in your arms, like right now, or as a casualty on the local news, that you wouldn't want to give

me a send-off to remember?"

"I'm saying, Richard, that...if you hypothetically go to war, we can hypothetically have sex."

The rain is pouring down on the pup tent, and Dick is laying on his back, and I'm there with my cheek against his chest, listening to his lungs exhaling, his heart thumping, his stomach turning over with creaks and groans. He flexes the muscles of his arms and abdomen until, gradually, his body relaxes, and I think he might be asleep.

"How about a hypothetical hand job?" he asks.

That boy goes to war, comes home alive, and gets what he is looking for, but not from me.

~

When the casino turns up nothing, we decide on the spur of the moment that we'll go and do something "cultural." The museum is close by, and it tells the extraordinary history of the Pequod, the tribe best known for their war with the Puritans of Massachusetts, and for sharing their name with Ahab's doomed ship. In the lobby, there is a teepee that allows patrons of the museum, two at a time, to huddle inside it and imagine themselves in the lives of the Indians. Peter and I wait in line together, unusually quiet and solemn, like the Indians we imagine ourselves to be. The two who go in before us are a young couple, and as they leave the teepee laughing about something naughty that they almost certainly did in there, there is a moment of oedipal distance between us.

Inside the teepee, there is a faint sound of drums wired in through speakers.

"So...why did you think Dad would be at Foxwoods?" Peter asks me, finally.

"I don't know," I say, "I just couldn't wait around at home. I'd go crazy."

He nods. "I understand."

No you don't, I want to say, *all you do is sit around at home.* But the last thing I would do is to start an argument with my son inside a teepee.

"What if this were our home?" Peter says, gesturing to the conical wood structure that surrounds us.

"Well, Honey, if this were our home, we'd be completely different people," I say, and Peter gives me a look, like he knows it's a dodge. "But even then I'd probably have to get out of the house now and then."

"That's what I'm saying," Peter says. "If this was home, we'd probably get out a whole lot more."

I smile, and put a hand on his shoulder. "Honey," I say, "You wouldn't last a day living in a teepee."

Peter takes out his phone, as though to prove my very point. "This would be so much easier if Dad owned a phone."

"He shouldn't even need a phone! This is crazy," I say. "How is it that I don't even know the first place he goes to when he runs away?"

Our time as Indians having elapsed, I lead Peter out of the teepee by his hand, into the gift store, where we handle little Indian erasers, little Indian keychains, little Indian salt and pepper shakers.

~

Ron treats Peter and me to the circus. The old-fashioned tent evokes turn-of-the-century carnivalia. Freakshows. Vaudeville. Ron is the perfect spectator. He laughs when the clowns walk out into the spotlight. He oohs and aahs at all the right places. He directs Peter to stage right and announces, "Look, the elephants are coming out!" My brother is avuncular without even trying.

As a kid, I remember, it was his goofiness that endeared him to me. Only a cornball like Ron would condescend to bring his kid sister along on his neighborhood romps, while he was supposed to be earning his bones as a local tough. When I started at the same school as him in the third grade (he was three years above me), he visited my class and, when the teacher's back was turned, stuck out his tongue at her. This made Ron the new Elvis.

But by the time I entered high school, I remember, his antics were embarrassing, juvenile—telling "jokes" that to me sounded racist and violent, like sublimated fantasies of genocide. We shared one year of high school, then Ron went to College down south, and found his roots as a Southern man. But, though he picked up the accent, the gentleman in

93

him didn't give birth full-term. When Peter was born, Ron bought me stuff—toys, flowers, equipment—that neither he nor I could afford. That was the kind of gentleman Ronald had become: a gentleman of gestures.

Now this is him, to my left, rubbing Peter's head until all his strands of hair stand up from friction. He has a firm handshake, and our Dad's whiskey habit, and a list of hobbies that announce his credentials as the "fun" uncle: surfing, snowboarding, and skydiving. This is Ron's vocabulary set, when talking about my husband: {boring, old, rich, snobby, dry, crusty, bland, spoiled, stiff}. This is John's, when talking about my brother: {null}.

~

We feel like the runaways now. The museum closes, and we just stick around, haunting the parking lot like tailgaters at a Dead concert. "What should we do?" I ask him, tugging his sleeve, getting too comfortable in my new role as the abandoned mother.

"What's open?" he asks.

"Just the casinos," I say.

Peter looks at his glowing flip phone. "It's eleven now. Let's go see Aunt Beth."

When we reach the casino floor, the prime-time crowd is gone, and they don't even card Peter for not being twenty-one enough. Beth is dealing out one patron, a tired old man with a stoop and a cane, when we join her. She talks to us like he's not even there.

"Sorry, no sign of John," she says with the practiced minimal dialogue of the blackjack table. Dealing cards must be the only profession where, the less the salesman says, the more the customer buys.

"That's okay, Beth. We're not looking for John anymore," I say, "Deal us in."

"Lay down your bets; minimum bets are $25; please leave your money or chips on the table," she says, and I smile at the banality of it.

We buy in, and Peter watches the cards hungrily. I'm looking up at Beth's face, which, with its lion quality, resembles John's.

"So, as a former social worker, doesn't this bother you at all?" I ask, gesturing at all the old, stooped, men and women at the surrounding tables.

"Blackjack is social work," she says, with a smirk.

Then the stooped old man next to us—thick glasses, thick New York accent—speaks up. "Lemme 'splain it this way: If you were trapped on a desert island with four strangers, and all you had was a deck of cards and the shirt on your back, what would you do?"

I'm trying to work out the metaphors. Is each table its own desert island, and the floor is the sea between them; or is the floor the desert, and each table a separate oasis? The difference, for some reason, is crucial to me.

"It sounds like a reality show," Peter observes out loud.

Beth scoffs. "They couldn't make a reality show out of this. On TV reality, people win prizes. In casino reality, they lose their mortgages, their wallets, and sometimes their sweethearts," she makes a brief, apologetic smile at me. "Sorry, Abby."

"Of course not," I say. "I'm just getting started."

Lay down your bets.

John and I agreed to abstain from sex for a whole month before the wedding. I came up with the idea on a spur-of-the-moment whim, over brunch at Rue De L'espoire, and to my surprise, John said "sure, let's try it." Try it? That was John: the sampler, the Patron-Saint of practicality and go-along spirit.

But the intersection of soul and body is the junction where physical comforts and stubborn morality collide—leaving, in its carnage, the carcasses of young love. A month without sex, and our relationship turned quiet, as though we feared our very voices could meet in the air and entwine themselves. In a perversion of the marriage vows, we had pitted our capacity for commitment against our need for one another.

Little things stuck to me like acupuncture pins, and I began to keep track of every trespass. John never socialized with any of his work friends, and suddenly they were throwing him a bachelor party? I seethed, as I am convinced any fiancée would, but I did not confront him, because such an argument could only end with some kind of compensatory pleasure, and then we would have proven to each other our failure to remain true to our intentions. So I asked my girlfriends to plan a send-off party for me too—a revenge party.

Man, we are pathetic in our heads.

When the bachelorette party got truly raunchy, I knew right away that Beth was the one to blame. None of my girlfriends from Vassar would even enter a strip club unless it was in my honor. It made me angry, at first, wondering if this was Beth's way of manufacturing secrets between us—a trump card in her back pocket, in case she ever needed to poison John against me. This is all I need on the day before I marry, I said sarcastically, more men.

But, starved of physical contact for weeks, surrounded by the barest presumption of modesty—a pair of boots underneath a bulging calf, a bowtie wrapped around a veined neck, a g-string unable to contain its rapidly swelling contents—I could hear the blood rush away from my head, into my legs, the bottom of my spine, my groin. Then, when the thin strips of cloth were thrown off, I was like a Henry Miller heroine, all sex.

My old roommate Lisa leaned over and said, "This is such a riot, Abby. Isn't this funny?"

The light from the lamppost is scattered across the windshield, casting dust shadows on the dash. I'm staring into the pattern it makes, with Peter's cell phone in my hand, in perfect stillness. Why am I hesitating?

Peter is asleep, reclined in the front passenger seat. A bag of junk from the museum gift shop is spilled on his lap. Penny artifacts.

At 4 a.m., finally, I make the call to Providence, and to my momentary surprise, John is back home. "Honey? What happened to you? Where are you?" I say, flustered, knowing it's a dumb question.

"There's something you need to know," he says, with an intensity that recalls my encounters, as a girl in college, with a series of passionate men who all suspected, deep down, that the world was an ornament crafted just for them. "I can still be cruel."

A pause. "John. You're not making sense right now."

"Did you read my letter?" he asks.

"Yes, we did," I say.

"Peter read the letter?" he says.

"Well, you *did* leave it on the kitchen table."

John sighs. "Okay, I just thought it was important for you to know...that I'm not a tamed animal, that I'm not a—"

"—okay. John? We're coming home," I say. And the sound of a quiet phone is like rain on the roof of a tent.

"Where are you?" he asks, and it occurs to me that I could say anything, anything at all.

"Never mind. Are you going to be home when we get there?" I ask. "Just, please, let me know either way."

"Yeah, I'll be here," he says, with either relief, or resignation.

The difference is crucial.

THE GOOD CHINA

Peter Gray

Peter's defense was passive. He held up his arms, stepped from side to side, and stood back from the offensive player, as though pantomiming an invisible wall.

He played basketball like it was baseball, John thought—hugging the space around the net like it was second base; running away from the other player, rather than getting in his face; always worried about being tagged.

John bunny hopped backward, and let the ball go in a perfect arc into the net.

"Eleven-four, you," Peter said, clearly more interested in ending the game.

"No, no," John said, scooping the ball from the ground and checking it back at his son, whose slight frame and made-for-basketball height resembled his own. "That was a walk. You have to call those, Pete." He flicked the basketball pole with his fingernail and the hollow, metallic sound lingered rudely. Whenever he came off of a lay-up, or a rebound, and found himself under the net, John always flicked the pole—counting coup on his opponent, turning an ordinary game of drivewayball into an all-out melee.

Peter dribbled the ball with his right hand, holding his left out loosely while his dad shuffled around him, stabbing the air with his hands, which, if nothing else, achieved the effect of distraction. Though already well behind the three-point line, Peter moved backward further, out of his dad's range, practically standing on the sidewalk, and took a shot. It fell short by a full yard, and John easily seized on the rebound. Ding!

But instead of ending their eleven-point game with a bank shot from the three-point line, as he was positioned to do, John moved in next to Peter, his elbow extended out, to block him. "C'mon, Dad. Let's finish this," Peter said.

"Why so eager to lose?" John said. He dribbled low to the ground, hunched over.

After teasing Peter with the ball for a while, John shouldered him out of the way for a lay-up, and the ball rolled off his fingers into the net. "Good game," said John.

"Yup," said Peter, starting to head inside, where his mother, Abigail, waved at them from the kitchen window. Peter waved back.

"Hold on," said John. "Stand next to me. I'm gonna teach you how to shoot."

"That's okay, I'm good," Peter said, lingering at the door.

"You're not good. That's why we gotta do this," John said to the back of Peter's head. Peter stood next to his dad, holding the ball. "This isn't baseball. Don't keep your eye on the ball. Keep one eye on the net, and one on the other guy. When you shoot, don't aim at the rim, aim just above the rim. And don't go for those lazy bank shots—"

"I got two of them past you," Peter reminded him.

"Don't brag; you're embarrassing yourself," John growled.

Peter tossed the ball with both hands, and it swirled around the rim before spilling over to the opposite side, where John caught it. "Don't shoot yet!" John said. "Listen to what I'm telling you. After the ball leaves your hands, you're not done with the shot. The most important thing is the follow-through. It doesn't matter where you're standing, or what kind of shot you are making. The most important thing is to follow through; otherwise, you have no control whatsoever. And the name of the game is control."

"Really? I thought it was basketball," Peter dead-panned.

"Smart-ass."

Recently, Abigail started volunteer work at the Center for the Disabled. The year before, she had tried building HUD houses, but found that, without experience, or at the very least body bulk, she was a mannequin on the construction site, modeling work clothes. She had been present for the groundbreaking, but hadn't even been back to that neighborhood since the building began. They offered her a secretarial role in the HUD office, but she couldn't imagine spending her time away from home in that way. If she was going to sit at a desk, she was going to get paid.

Abigail found her work at the Center for the Disabled more

fulfilling on a personal level. At the CFD, she was physically useful to many people, several times a day. When Richard, a man in a wheelchair, passing her in the hallway, dropped his book on the tile floor, Abigail leaned over to pick it up for him.

"Thanks," he said.

"*Hamlet?*" Abby asked.

"Can you believe I'm reading it for the first time?" he said. He was the director of the CFD theater troupe. "I've been around for sixty years and never read *Hamlet*."

The troupe was practicing to perform *Rosencrantz and Guildenstern are Dead*. The director's name was Richard, like the Shakespearean king, a fact which the troupe exploited on days when he was behaving particularly monarchical. He was one of the less disabled members— they are called "members," Abigail noted, as if the CFD were an exclusive country club—so he helped organize events and activities, and acted somewhat like a staff member himself.

A group of seven less-disabled members had been putting on productions in the summers for a number of years, and somewhere along the line had committed exclusively to Shakespeare, and Shakespeare-related plays. Originally, the performances were just weekend entertainment for the most severely disabled members, but then, when members began to invite their families, and family members began to invite friends, it became a community staple—an anticipated public event. They started to sell tickets, so that when Abigail got involved, during the Fifth CFD Summer Shakespeare Festival, it was also a cash cow.

"The ending isn't a happy one, I'm afraid," Abigail said. "Everyone dies."

"I like that," Richard said, and smiled like he'd just heard a bit of good news. "Just like real life."

With his wife away from home three evenings a week, John lapsed into a regressive bachelorhood. He still shouldered his share of the housework, which consisted of lifting himself up long enough to put the trash out by the curb, but other household things were left unfinished; even, occasionally, the cooking. Sometimes it was too much of an effort to make food. Sometimes it was too small a reward

101

to eat it.

Taking out the trash, John began to realize, was what he contributed to the family labor. Even Peter—who, ever since school ended, had made a suspiciously successful effort to avoid going out to eat at the diner with his high school friends—managed to leave the dishes in the dishwasher after dinner, where they waited for Abigail to turn the machine on at night. But taking out the trash—that was John's business.

Sometimes he woke up early and watched as the trash truck emptied his two mismatched aluminum bins, the way Abby used to watch Peter and Anila, eight years apart, mount the steps of a bus every morning. He tried to construct in his mind what Abby was doing now. The best he could muster was a blurry image of Abby sweeping the stage, dusting the props, and making sandwiches for the actors.

When Abigail first began volunteering, it had sounded to John like a decent thing to do with her time. Then, when it began to intrude on their personal life, John started thinking of the idea of working without pay as slightly offensive. When he thought about it now, it was almost an insult, for a man who had worked his whole life to maintain an upper-middle class salary, to have his wife go off and work for nothing. As though she were subtly communicating to him that the way he spent his days was worthless, a hobby, just another way to pass the time.

At first, Abigail was flattered that the troupe was trying so hard to draft her onto the stage. But then, though she hated herself for thinking it, she was also horrified by how easily they assumed she would fit in. It was a paralyzing thought, that this was the company to which she belonged—a company of the slightly less disabled.

Abigail was never involved in drama—had never been in a play, even in grade school. Once, in her last year of college, she fell abysmally in love with an actor named Connor, going so far as to move in with him, against the advice of her parents. He had a tortured childhood—a topic to which he could steer any conversation— including one story that he often repeated about a crazy religious mother who burned things, which Abby assumed to be apocryphal.

He had a drug habit that made him even more aloof, and therefore more enticing to her, at that age. In those days, Abigail saw her quiet tolerance of her circumstances as heroic, and it was not until Connor invited his ex-girlfriend to live with them in their apartment that her heroism was tested, and found wanting.

After leaving Connor's apartment—that very day in fact—Abby met John at the public library, and was so startled by his uprightness, his maturity, that she promised herself in that moment she would marry him if he ever asked. She needed to be good to herself, she decided. She needed to find a good man, for a change, and then to hold on to him. So she was stunned when he asked her to marry him, that very week, over brunch at the Rue de L'Espoire. It was a fancy-casual French restaurant (they served duck, but they also kept ketchup on the tables).

She didn't understand quite why, but it was this same feeling that struck her now, as she debated whether to join the troupe of the slightly less disabled. That she ought to do so. That it would be good for her.

Driving home with the sun still high in the sky unsettled him. It was seven in the evening, and John felt a vague desire to drive around a while before returning home. Night, at least, would have presented the day with a choice of finality. But driving home from the office with the sun still piercing through the windshield, after working a solid block of ten hours with no natural light, he could no longer pretend to be lost. The path home was too clear.

First, he reviewed the events of the day in his head, and chastised himself for all the little things he'd left undone. Then, finding Peter napping on the living room sofa, he felt his son's idleness as a rebuke to him. John stood looming over him, his suit jacket folded over his arm, for longer than he needed in order to ascertain that Peter was sleeping. Several things occurred to John at that moment: that standards of living are on the decline; that he wished he could sleep all afternoon; that he would not be able to use the sofa to watch television or read the paper (which he'd left unfinished from that morning, anticipating the moment when he would arrive home from work to an empty couch).

John had the habit of yelling, and apologizing immediately, before Abigail even realized that she had been yelled at. It was a marital habit—complicated, evolved, and bearing no resemblance to behavior that he would have exercised in other circumstances.

As Abigail slipped out of her clothes and into bed, she asked John why, in all their years of marriage, he hardly ever talked about his family. He shrugged. Then, after a durable silence, she asked whether he had called the phone company about a questionable charge on their bill. He acted as though provoked. "Look, I may be old, but I'm not senile. Gimme a break. You're not so young either," then slid seamlessly into the apology. "I'm sorry, baby. Come 'ere." And Abigail would let herself be held, feeling whiplashed by the change in mood.

Her friend Jen, the armchair psychologist, had unofficially diagnosed John as bipolar. But Jen used bipolar to describe anything with contrasts. The decor in their house was said to be bipolar. Her manual shift Volvo. The modern world. The Old Testament God.

"She has got to find a new adjective," Abby remembered thinking at the time, but wondered too whether, in just this one instance, it might not be appropriate.

The basement door—the door that led to Peter's underground bedroom—opened, and he heard footsteps walking down the stairs. With no guests at all that summer, he wasn't accustomed to hearing footsteps on the stairs. His dad leaned over the railing. His hair was flecked gray, and his chin was glistening with aftershave. He wore a suit jacket and tie. It was always a surprise to see his father in the morning, fully awake. As though he embodied a different possibility of who he might have been.

"Make a plan," his dad said.

"Huh?" His eyebrows raised, Peter looked up from his book.

"Don't be thick, Pete. You heard me." John began to walk back up the stairs.

"Dad?" Peter was so disoriented, between reading Vasari's *Lives of the Artists* one moment, and being brow-beaten by his father's anger the next, that he literally felt dizzy. John paused on the steps. "Uh... can we talk about it?"

"What's there to talk about? You're not going to live in the basement all your life. So you might as well start now. Just make a plan, and follow through with it. It doesn't matter what you do, as long as you stick with it long enough to carry it out. You know what I'm saying?"

Peter stared at his dad as though he didn't, in fact, know what he was saying. He hadn't dressed or brushed yet, so he lay there skinny in his boxers and tee, and he had a fuzzy look to him that looked stoned. "Do you want me to find a job?" Peter said.

"Hey, there's a plan!" John walked down the stairs and leaned on the railing.

"But where would I work?"

"Peter. I'm only gonna say it twice. It doesn't matter what you do, so long as you do it, and follow through with it."

John and Abby sat on opposite sides of the bed, half-turned toward each other—an awkward pose that looked like two nudes modelling. It was three a.m. on the digital clock, and they had been talking, without facing each other, since ten.

"I'll move out," John said.

"No, you wouldn't adjust well," Abigail said. "Let me find an apartment. I've seen a few places along Blackstone Boulevard I wouldn't mind renting."

John sniffed. "I forgot about Blackstone Boulevard." Only the year before, they had purchased a burial plot along that same wide street, which bordered the river.

"It's not like we have to sell everything. Actually, I'm kind of looking forward to living on a tighter budget. It'll be like college."

John cast her a hurt look, which she either ignored, or didn't notice.

That night, they had said the things that they'd spent years trying not to say. Abby was trailer trash. John was a robot. Abby was just like her mom, acting proud when she had nothing to be proud about. John had tedious habits and no energy leftover from work for his family. Her ambitions to save the world were laughable. His moods were worse than a premenstrual teenager.

When John first began dating Abigail, he should have known it wouldn't last. The last twenty-six years, he figured now, were borrowed years. She had a touched quality, a hovering-above-life smile. In an odd way, John thought, it had always been the agreement—they raised children together, until the children were no longer children. At which point the contract on their marriage would be reviewed. The way she carried herself said she had never "settled"—not really. It was only luck that he had met her coming off of a bad relationship with an actor. Now, he figured, she was simply cashing in on what fate had promised. He was almost excited for her—for what she might do next in her life—except that he hated the thought of Abby alone. Or worse, of Abby not alone.

John began throwing things away as though he had a vendetta against common household objects. Anything that he couldn't remember using in the last year, he disposed of, regardless of value. He decided that they only needed two of each dish in the house, so he purged the house of its excess dish ware, including the good china—a wedding gift from Abby's brother.

He had thrown away so much, he thought, it should be easy to keep track of what was left. He set to cataloguing the objects in his house, marking what belonged to whom, and where it could be of most use. When it came to clothes, John suddenly couldn't tell what belonged to his son, and what to him.

He found a desk set that he bought for Peter when he was fourteen, but never used. John himself had been impressed by how compact it was. How little space it occupied. He took it out of the shrink wrap, and fastened a nib to the tip of the pen.

He decided to compose a letter to his wife, which he could only recall doing once or twice before throughout their marriage. It felt awkward, writing "Dear Abby..." as if John were one among thousands of letter-writers, clamoring for her advice.

John wrote that he wished he could take back the things he said, and that he wished he could learn to communicate. He wrote that he knew now why she always asked about his dead relatives. At the time, he mistook it for a morbid curiosity, but now he thought she may have wanted some assurance, that if she were to suddenly drop off, someone would still remember, and talk about, *her*. So he wrote to her about his family.

He wrote about his grandfather, who came to Providence from Corsica on a rickety boat, and became the first Italian millionaire in New England, recycling paperboard before anybody knew what recycling was. About his dad who became the first of his family to go to college, brokered for a while, invested his money in stocks, bonds, start-up companies (some good, some bad), and left John with just enough to raise a family on. About how John himself never had a head for business, and decided as a last resort that civil engineering is something he could live with. "Once in a while," he wrote, "I get to see a dam or bridge that I helped engineer, and it's almost like I built it myself."

He ended with, "In a month, our son is going off to school and studying art. To be an artist. At art school. I don't think he or Anila will ever have children of their own. But, then again, at least he's doing something. I just wish that something didn't mean the end of the Gray family line, our prosperity. New money, old money, no money. That's what's become of our generations."

But he tore it up before sending it. He laughed at how pathetic it was to write a letter in the modern world.

Abigail drove through Silver Lakes. Her big brother Ron—the kind of old-school, unapologetic racist one never sees these days—used to call this neighborhood "The Swamp" because, he said, of all the "mud people" who lived there. Blacks, browns, and yellows. This was going to be her neighborhood soon. She stayed on Blackstone Boulevard just long enough to make John comfortable. Now, she wanted to be close to the culture. "Culture," Ron reminded her over the phone, "is what they call it when they grow mold in a dish."

On the way to her new apartment, she passed the HUD house she had almost helped build. It was flat-topped and squat. It had one bush and one window. All she could think about was how happy she was not to have taken part in the building of such an ugly house. Sure, somebody would call it home. But it looked to her like a social security building. Something functional, designed by engineers. Utterly indifferent to beauty.

Instead of going to RISD, John's son went to a no-name art college in San Francisco. Here they were in Providence, sitting on the same hill with the best art and design school in the country, and his son found something obscure and far away instead.

Respecting his mother's request to call his father on his birthday at least, Peter picked up the phone and dialed home. Jockeying the call home hadn't been the same since his parents had split up. There was no Mom to buffer the silences between them. No one to pass the phone to.

"Hello?"

"It's Peter."

"Well, hello. How the hell are you?"

"Fine, I guess. Starting a new class this week. Busy, busy, busy."

"That right? So, what is busy, for an artist?" John smiled like it hurt. Peter could hear the smile, the angles of the mouth drawn up and held there.

"It's strange. You wouldn't think art is such hard work, but it is physically exhausting."

"Yeah, you've never been all that physical," John said. "You must get tired easy."

"I'm physical all the time now. It's hard work, which I didn't expect."

"Yeah, your sister is the physical one. You've always been mental," John said.

A pause. "I'm physical," Peter said, "when I want to be."

"Nah," said John. "Anila is physical."

"I'm physical." Though no one was around to see it, he grabbed a fistful of his shirt fabric, as though assuring himself, at least, of his own physicality.

"Keep it up and you might convince yourself," John said.

"Whatever, Johnny," Peter said, "you know me better than I do, I guess."

"Hold on, now. Don't back away from that. Defend what you said. You made a point: now prove it. What do you do that's so physical?" John waited, and the silence on the line dragged.

"No, you're absolutely right, everything you were just saying."

It all came together at once. The indecisiveness, the passivity, and

108

the sheer yieldingness of him. He found it hard to differentiate his flaws from those of his son. It hardly mattered whose, now that Peter was grown.

"You know what the problem with you is, Pete?" John's grimace turned into a pugnacious overbite. "I never smacked you when you were a kid. If I had hit you more, you wouldn't have such a loose fucking attitude."

"Wait a minute," Peter said, letting the anticipation linger. "If you're the one who didn't hit me enough, isn't that really a problem with you?"

"Don't tempt me. I'm still your father. I'm not above hitting you. I don't care if you are twenty fucking years old and living in a loft."

"Okay…so you're gonna fly out to San Francisco and physically beat me?" Peter tried to laugh, but it came out a snort.

"Don't think I won't," said John. He could feel his face go red. He had the look of a tormented boy facing a childhood enemy.

"Okay, Dad, I'll see you in California." He pushed the off-button on his touchtone. On a cordless phone, hanging up the line was so unsatisfying.

This year, the troupe went back and did *Hamlet*. But there were no young volunteers. Richard, at sixty-two years old, had to play the role of Hamlet himself. It was strange at first to see an old man agonizing over his fate, privy to so much doubt, wringing his hands over a simple choice. When a ghost appears in your life and says, "Avenge me," at sixty, you ought to know whether you are going to act on it or not.

Even though she had seen it rehearsed at least twice a week all summer, there was a moment, on opening night, when Abby fell fully under the spell of the play. Before an audience of the King, Hamlet was prompting the players to recite a speech describing the fatal battle between Pyrrhus and Priam, at the height of the siege of Troy, when the peaceful but decadent Trojans, after a decade of war, are finally overrun by the barbarian Achaeans, and their king quartered twice—that is, cut into eighths—by Pyrrhus.

The whole production was aimed at unnerving Claudius, the murderer king, upon whom Hamlet was destined to take revenge.

But in that moment, before his vengeance could be consummated, there was the Prince of Denmark, putting on a play to inspire the king's guilt, rather than running him through with his saber.

Somehow, speaking from his wheelchair gave Richard latent strength—as though, no matter how much passion he put into his performance, he was holding more in reserve.

As the scene ended, Richard spoke in a voice which was simultaneously a yell and a whisper: "The play's the thing / Wherein I'll catch the conscience of the king!"

The performance was so stirring to Abby, she wished for the first time in a long time that her family was all of one piece, if only long enough to watch this play together.

From the window of the plane, John could barely see the peaks and valleys on the surface. The notorious hills of San Francisco seemed barely raised from the rest of the topography, like goose bumps.

On the west coast of America—Peter had said when he first moved there—San Francisco is the closest thing to Providence. He kept referring to its "culture," and the "culture" of Providence, and John couldn't help wondering if he'd meant something other than the local museums. They were both "hip," he'd said, and "progressive." John thought there was something euphemistic about this praise.

As he arrived in the airport lobby—passing, in his first five minutes off the plane, a hare krishna, a thin man with multiple piercings, and what looked like a transvestite—John caught a glimpse into what must be his son's notion of progress.

When he had first moved into the studio, earlier that year, the first thing Peter did was to call his Mom. He sounds just like a young man, Abigail thought, as she listened over the phone. Peter couldn't stop talking about the cities he'd lived in. He just couldn't get over the fact of his independence. "That's wonderful, dear," Abigail found herself saying, and thought also of how she must sound just like an old woman.

What he talked about was how kindred their two cities were, yet how different. "San Francisco is, like, a guy who used to write poetry as a teenager, now about to turn thirty, and is looking for something practical—like computers. Providence is this old man who worked in a factory his whole life, who just discovered that there's poetry in him after all."

Abigail had laughed. "I wish there were more men like that," and added parenthetically "Then we wouldn't have any problems casting for this play."

There was no doorman, no gate, no locks on the door, even.

The studio was wide open, to let in the less-stale air of the hallway. Peter shared the place with two roommates, both of whom were sitting on the couch while Peter shook around in front of them like a fool. They were playing charades, and from John's vantage all the gesturing looked like a mating dance.

Peter looked up, and they briefly made eye contact. John had a lot of expectations: that his son would fight back, that his son would win; that the father would slink off back to Rhode Island like an aging lion. That, maybe, Peter would placate him. What he did not expect was the look of utter surprise on Peter's face. It did not seem possible to him, after twenty years of being a child in his father's house, that Peter would still doubt his word.

As he pulled back for the punch, John swallowed a morsel of air that felt like a hard candy gone down by accident. He used this choking sensation to drive his momentum. There was an instant, so brief that it seemed to contain no time at all, that John could have softened the blow. But at that point, what was there to do? At the very least, he wanted his son to be proud of his strength. He followed through with the shot, connecting at the jaw line, and sent Peter cringing to the ground—dazed, bruised, and half-coiled up on the floor. He raised his hands to cover his face. He shook his head from side to side. He continued to speak in gestures.

The flight home was faster—blurry, less sequential—more like a montage, as John fluttered in and out of awareness of his surroundings. He looked out of the window; there was no view at night. There was something uneasy about the plane. A lot of missing seats, which meant travelers were staying home instead—had changed plans, had decided not to fly, even after paying for tickets. John stared at all the empty seats wondering, "Who? Who would ever do such a stupid thing?"

220 Nickels

Gee McBock

Pigeon-shit. This whole damn city. The rain coming down and all of it. So I'm standing under an awning looking out. As if I'm the one the world's protecting. While all the walking people hold up their mushroom tops, and dodge puddles.... Rain drums on the canvas cover. Water slides off the canopy. Full streams come down, like men are pissing off the rooftop. The darker it gets, the brighter it looks inside, and warmer too. Think of all the places it says "rest" but you can't rest there. Restroom. Rest stop. Restaurant. State comes out and tells me I'm owed restitution. Says I need to get some restitution.

Asics comes up to me later and says, "Reebok, you on patrol tonight?"

So I say, "Yup," because that's how it is.

"A'right." He says.

"Whassat mean?" I ask.

He says, "Nothin'." Then, "Reebok. You just a dirty trash-picker. Look at you. Why don't you wash them clothes, it's raining out. Shit." He'd got fired from his work, so something was biting his nuts that day.

"Trucks run all night. Won't let it get wasted, for Chrissakes. You have a smoke, Asics?" I give him my hand like he should fill it. He looks at it like it had ants crawling on it. Then he starts laughing.

"Why you call me Asics, Reebok? You the shoe man. Reebok. Look at your raggedy shoes, Reebok. Reebok."

"Man—you call me Reebok, I call you Asics. You call me by my right name, and I'll do too." I said.

"That's your right name." He said. "Reebok."

"No it fuckin' ain't." I say. "It's McBock. It's Irish, you dumb fuck."

Asics starts laughing through his teeth, holding up his hand to stop the spittle. He's convulsing like it's the funniest thing he heard all day. "Reebok." He repeats.

"Gimme a smoke, Ron." I say, only to shut him up. The rain's died by now.

"Get your own smokes, Reebok. I ain't your 7-11." And Asics guns it, heading for the commuter parking lot where I guess his van is.

That's how the night started. And things might not have been the way they've been since then if he hadn't been so damn tight-assed with his cigarettes.

~

All the good junk is underneath the bad junk. Some folks think it must all be good to us, since they didn't want any of it. Like it's no good to them so it's no good to anybody. Like we're just pretending it's all good, but it's all real bad. But I know for sure some junk is good and other junk is bad.

Folks are throwing away playing cards, ropes, hangers, and clothes with the zippers still on 'em; things like wood chairs and coffee tables, and bike parts; and you don't know how many cans. Because it's me that counts 'em up. How many did I get that night Asics came up to me and said he wouldn't give me none of his cigarettes? Two hundred and twenty. Nickels. A wardrobe of used clothes. A wash and a cut. A month's permit for cold water and ice. A bus ticket to Portland.

And some people out here won't go to the missions for food. They'll collect day-old bread and sardines and all else. They hoard. The smart ones won't hoard, and won't starve either. Just take it from the Christians cause that's what they're there for. Anything else is stupid. You just don't believe all they say and start spreading the word. Wind up on Washington Street. A sign in your hand instead of a hat.

There's something sad about folks that try hard. Look what they pit themselves against. The night. The cold. I'll throw my dice with the dead. Outer space always wins. It's everywhere and they're not.

But when you give up life, that's when you're strongest. I know not because that's what I do but because that's what I see…. Lemme 'splain about Red. Red saved. Got his last ticket to Boston, and jumped off a bridge into the Charles River. Doctors wrapped his broken bones and put him out on the street again. He got a care-about-nothing job, running errands for dope-dealing kids. Some

114

hired goombahs smacked him around. He cut them up with a scalpel he'd took from the hospital. Later he was picked up. Asked to take the job of the men he killed. Turned bouncer for a club. Now he runs that fuckin' club. The old owner got put out on the street. And all Red did was different was give up.

Now the night is blue as it gets. Cats snarl and screw in the dark. Roots creep up the sidewalk cracks. Rain settles on the street. Now the late-comers scavenge all I missed or left behind.

Now what?

Now the canopy is dry. I make a seat of it. My pocket full of rice crackers someone thought they'd throw away a full bag. Chewing on crumbs. A few hard nuggets are like rocks, and I spit 'em. Keep checking in my other pocket for my nickels. Pieces of metal. In thirty years I only found one with an Indian on it. And when you run your thumb over his face it doesn't feel any different from other nickels.

Soon as Ron got a job and a car he was better than us. He finished school and now the rest of us was ignorant. But I'm the one who knows nickels. It's Thomas Jefferson's head on most of them. He's turning to the right—his right, my left. That ain't his real hair. The words around him are Latin.

Maybe Ron could show up on time and deliver mail. But that's a fool's game. Same as shouting Jesus on a street corner. At least those guys won't hoard—they'd give you a cigarette if they had one. But Ron didn't. Otherwise I'd be down on the canal watching the water move and chewing on a butt. But 'cause of Ron I'm waiting around in the city, nothing to smoke. Hell I went to school too. But something kept nudging me outside. I used to hear someone calling me out. Really hear him.

Now the cleaners come out. Stubby trucks swishing foam, skirting the curbs. Moving in figure eights. Chasing dogs. Cruel sons of bitches.

Now the runners check their wristwatches. Now the TV switches on in some second-story apartment. Now a bald man in flannel heaves the trash out the door. The last one. He heard the trash trucks beeping and probably tumbled out of his bed into the night. A lump of sugar in black coffee. Goes back to bed.

Now I get down from my seat and poke over to the green bin. What's he left in there that he had to get out this morning? Pile of diapers. Yeah. There's good junk and bad junk.

Now another junk-finder is down the road, and I see her pull out a radio. I'm walking over and she's tugging on something. Must be all kinds of stuff in there. The stuff is so heavy, she pushes the bin on its side and mines it out with a stick. Cappuccino machine. Food processor. Humidifier. Video players. Blenders. Everything connected to wires. She takes the radio. Looks at me like I'm cursed. Leaves the bin toppled there with its guts exposed.

I find an empty can in it. It's no good for nickels I know. But It'd do for trade. Leisure Soda, it says. And there is some sticker says "Trinity Theater" on it. Myron would want it. It's just the thing Myron would want.

Voices come up, and first I try to wave 'em away. But this time they are calling me inside. This house. Its pillars. Ivy and brick. With the trash full of dead objects. Its door stands open and a voice calls out through the screen. "Come 'ere." It says. "Come on. Come 'ere." I step up, then back again, then up the steps. Man is always curious.

A full-robed body appeared in the screen, and I step back from it.

"No. Come 'ere." It says. "Come on inside." It holds open the screen and beckons. I've only been asked inside a house twice before. The first I was fed. The second I was beaten. Both times I heard the voice but both times it was calling me out. Never in. Now I listened.

Now what?

I'm not so dumb I don't know what a palace looks like. The place is gilded. Paintings take up space on every wall. But who can make out what this man-boy is, or what it wants?

It says, "What were you doing out there?" Its voice deeper than at first. Now I see it's a man, but careful and soft like a baby.

"I'm…" But I don't get it out before I see Man has a gun on the table by him. Next to a vase of cut flowers. Man isn't trying to feed me either. "jus' walkin' by." I reach for the screen door.

"Could you stay a minute?" He asks.

"Why?" Something holds me there between in and out, though I know I should go out. I don't need no voices to tell me so.

"You seem like someone a man can trust." He says.

"Hey, you want your can back—" I start fishing around in my coat pockets.

"No. Don't." He says. "I threw it away; it's yours now. I'm more interested in your company."

"I ain't a queer, if that's what you're asking." I say.

"No!" He says defensively, and he looks hurt almost. "Nothing like that."

"Then what do you want me for?" I ask, one hand still on the door.

"Because I don't know who you are. And I don't care." He says.

I start to say, "I'm Gee Me—"

"I don't care!" he shouts. Stuns me quiet. He closes the door and sits down. Motions for me to sit too. Then he softens. Leans in toward me like I was somebody important. "Could you do something for me, Gee?"

My retort comes in a little on the delay. "You know, I don't care who you are either, Man." I say.

"Good." Man says. And hands me the trigger side of his revolver. "Could you shoot me in the face, then?"

"Fuck, man. Naw—" I try to shove it back.

"Wait, please!" He takes hold of my fist, awkwardly clasping his gun. He puts it right against his forehead.

I almost pull the trigger, just to shut him up. I can't stand people whining at me. Like when I'm hanging around the library. People's kids are screaming and making a fuss. I almost lose it. Then with the gun it's like bad thoughts are a twitch away from killing thoughts.

"No damn way." I say.

"Please. You can have everything I own. I don't want it. Just fuckin' shoot me."

"I wouldn't want your stuff if it was free. It's all bad junk. I sure as hell ain't gonna fuckin' shoot somebody for it." I tell him.

"You're serious." He says. "You're serious?"

"I can't use any of your shit." I tell him, again.

"Nothing? You don't want any of it? Nothing?" He says it so many times, it loses meaning. "Nothing? Nothing?" His hand relaxes some, and I let go of the gun as best I can. Now he holds it in his hand pointed back at himself.

I look around a little bit. I don't see nothing I want. "Nope."

"What about this?" He points at the big TV with his free hand, while his trigger hand fumbles with the backwards gun.

I shrug. "What the hell am I gonna do with that?"

When he finally gets the pistol pointed at me, he tells me to walk up the stairs. He'll follow. Up in his room he shows me ornaments, heirlooms, treasures, antiques. Things dirty with memory. "I guess those be worth something to somebody, but I don't know who'd want 'em. I sure as hell don't need 'em." I say.

He takes me into his office. Computers, monitors like big robot heads, printers, disks, scanners, drives—all flood the place, fill every groove. That stuff is some of the worst bad junk you can find. I tell him as much.

He keeps opening and closing doors, leading me into rooms stocked with stuff he holds onto greedily with his eyes, as if they were whores in a harem. Last he brings me into the basement, where I guess he molds and paints because there is brown clay and colored spots everywhere. Sculptures, nudes of women mostly, some crazy shapes I don't know what.

He stands in the center of the room looking at me. Trying to read my face. He expects something. I hate people looking at me like that.

"Nothing?" He asks. I shrug, and he starts for the stairs.

"Wait. What about those?" I ask, showing him a box in the corner of his studio. It's filled with old frames. Some with dusty glass in the middle. Some void. But the wood is still good, and they hold together okay.

He looks down at the frames, then up at me.

"Wha...are you an artist?" He asks me.

"Nope." I say. "I'm just saying what about those. I'd take those... but I wouldn't kill you for 'em. Just if you were getting rid of them."

"Why those?" He insists.

I can't answer him right away.

"I could use those." I say.

He stands there a long time. But I'm patient too. So finally he says, "Take 'em."

Man follows me up from the basement. Gun dangles loosely in his hand. My arms full with boxes.

When we get up there, I look at him full in the eyes. His face is pinched. He has the look of a man who stayed up all night standing in front of a mirror, and didn't find nothing he liked. Strange, thinking we'd both been awake all night on the same trash day. Except instead of an old canopy, he sat under a roof next to his cut flowers. And instead of looking out on the corner park, he stared into his own babyish face. I pause at the screen door, where I entered.

"I want somethin' else too." I say, holding out a hand. I balance the frames on my side. Resigned, he places his pistol there. I drop it into the box, and carry it out.

I already told you how Red made it. I pass his club, The Manhattan Project, in the downcity. Now some guy who wears robes and slippers, some guy who owns his own piece of this earth, got saved from himself and maybe lives for another thirty years or so. What's he gonna do that Red couldn't even do? And what does that do for me? How can I lift myself out if I haven't given up, but I don't want nothing either? I mean, I've got the gun, and probably more balls to use it than Man did.

On the way to Myron's, I start to see messages all over the place. Not only to me, but written for everyone—little voices in ink, or chalk. One of them is a sign, someone had scratched off the last word, so it says "Do not." So I hang a frame on that one.

Some street-paver has written some code on the asphalt, that I can't make sense of. A girl made a little hopscotch game on her driveway. Two teenagers are remembered in wet cement: JF heart GG. Graffiti names tag the brick sides of pharmacies and liquor stores. Someone's spilled coffee landed, it looks like, in the shape of a pig. A telephone pole covered with dozens of stickers, each one announcing some event, long gone now.

I start to hang frames everywhere, or lay them all over the place, I have so many of 'em. Until I get to Myron's diner. He's the same age as me. He used to put food out from his restaurant. And I brought him cans—he only wanted the odd ones, for his collection. The rest I traded in for nickels. I leave the can of Leisure Soda on the steps up to the Backdrop Café. And I put my last frame around it.

I'm about to leave the box too. Until I see the silver glint of the handle, and remember that gun Man gave me. I pick it up. Feel its heft. Thinking maybe I should go back and see Red. Get my old job back. It's come morning. A siren sounds. I haven't slept all night so I figure maybe I'm just imagining it. But in the sheen of the diner— the reflective gloss that covers that silver capsule—blue and red lights spiral and wheel. The surface isn't perfect. It dulls and cakes with time. Wear. Exhaust. Pigeon-shit.

The Ballad of John Gray

John Gray

John's daughter, Anita, grew up in the seventies, when none of the teddy bears talked and none of the toys had buttons. John's son, Peter, though, was a child of the eighties, and every toy he owned, it seemed, had a minicomputer, an internal mechanism that, when exposed, looked like a bomb. And there was an entire year of John's life (when Peter was two years old) that he seemed to keep hearing a particular guitar-shaped toy play "It's a Small World" on a permanent loop. It was Petey's favorite toy, which he carried with him everywhere, and there was nothing John could do, short of quitting his family for good, to avoid that insipid song.

Often, now, as John is riding to work or going over the budget, that song will come upon him unawares, and he will be seized with a sudden urge to take apart every computer within range of his screwdriver. The space that the song occupies in his head is far out of proportion with what it merits, but it is, to John's infinite dismay, the fastest-growing property there. When he is alone, and the first strains of the chorus begin, John will literally hit himself in the head. But brute force will not exorcise the demon.

John is having trouble staying focused. The monitor wavers in his sight, the clean lines of the diagram look bent. Only his hand moves, in small circles, palm cupping the mouse, finger tapping on the button. His pupils shift slowly one way, then reset to their original position, like typewriter tape. Suddenly, the image on the browser window is blocked by an error message that reads, "You are disconnected."

"Damn," John says, not angry, but incantatory, as though repeating the name of a stranger to whom he has just been introduced. John finds that he is cursing, not the computer, but himself, for the poor presentation he gave that morning, which was attended by the

121

President of Benson Control, a man who holds John's professional future in his hands, and only visits the Boston office twice a year.

Increasingly, John is finding his emotional responses to be on time-delay. He remembers saying something awful (though he can't remember what) to his wife Abigail last week, and now he feels suddenly ashamed. He bought a boat in a company charity event two months ago (what is he going to do with a boat anyway?), and now he feels nostalgic for that party where everyone took turns congratulating him and asking if he was going to invite them all out on his new boat. And just now, John felt the first pang of embarrassment over his missteps in the boardroom hours ago.

The screen is frozen, not responding to his clicks. He jerks the mouse around the pad (on which is laser-stitched a picture of a sunny beach in Bermuda), to no effect. He repeatedly presses the enter key. Enter, Enter, Enter, Enter. The computer beeps, but does not respond. He presses down and holds the escape button. Escape... But neither button—enter or escape—works.

John's office looks out, on one side, at the Providence skyline, where the summer heat is carrying off the clouds. Through the opposing window, he can see the cubicle-dwellers, who, through the sound-proofed glass, are like characters on a muted television soap opera.

John waits. A row of silver balls, suspended from a black frame, click back and forth on his desk—have been clicking back and forth all day—like fat kids on swings crashing into each other again and again and again.

~

John stands and leaves the office, shutting the door gently behind him. Whenever John stands up in that office it seems to him as though he has been sitting in the center of a maze. Sharp corners point at you, mirrors trick you into seeing yourself in two places at once, and the utter monotony of color and form converge to defeat your sense of getting anywhere at all. Sound gets trapped in them too and, walking through a long row of offices, what you can hear is just so many taps on a keyboard, the sawing of a printer, a whisper into the telephone, a shuffling of papers, a curse, and that is all you know of those people.

John brushes past the teflon maze of wall partitions. Phones buzz here and there like mating birds.

"Hi, Phil," John says, pausing beside one of the cubicles, which, in contrast with the stark and colorless work stations of other Benson employees, is gaudy with stickers, bobble-heads, fuzzy dice, and other tchotchkes. Phil wears a striped button-down and polka-dot tie, with black-framed glasses and hair that looks wet.

"Hi, John. How can I help?"

"Nothing big. Just computer trouble," John says.

Phil scoffs. "Computer trouble isn't nothing, my friend. How are you going to work without a computer?"

"I can't. That's why I need your help. Come on," John waves Phil over to his office, doing his best to act chummy with the staff.

Phil waits just long enough to allow John to wonder if he was going to offer his help at all. Then he follows John to his office.

"What system are you working on?" Phil asks.

John realizes that, for all the time he spends in front of a computer, he has no idea what "system" he is on.

"I…don't know," he admits, as he sits down at his desk.

Phil scoffs again.

"Phil, could you not do that?" John says, rubbing his temples with his forefingers.

"Sorry," Phil says, sensing his boss' fragile mood.

Phil sits hunched at John's computer, tapping in one line of code after another. John rarely invites coworkers into his office, and feels Phil's presence as a kind of invasion. And he seems to be taking a long time.

To break the silence, John asks, "Did you ever have a song in your head that just repeated over and over again, and seemed like it would never go away?"

Phil cocks an eyebrow. He is the sort of man who takes pride in the way he can raise an eyebrow, the sort who practices it before a mirror. "An ear worm? Sure. Happens all the time. Right now you know what I got stuck in my head?"

"What?" John asks.

"Nevermind. You don't want to know."

"Yes, I do," John says. "Tell me."

"Okay." Phil closes his eyes as though singing in the shower, and belts out in a false-falsetto, "I am a man who will fight for your honor. I'll be the hero that you're dreaming of..." He looks up, for reaction. Instead of laughter, John's face registers something closer to horror. "It's the theme from *Karate Kid*. You seen it?"

"How do you get rid of an ear worm?" John asks.

"Easy," says Phil. "Listen to another song; or even better, sing a song yourself over and over again. What I do, sometimes, is just make up my own nonsense song, because nonsense lyrics are the most infectious. Want to hear my latest one?" Without pausing for approval, Phil gets into a wide-legged heavy-metal stance and sings out, "Fly my baby away, she say, I don't wanna go there, yeah. Tell me where, I swear, I won't say nuthin. Do it agin, huah! Do it again, huah!"

~

Every morning, John takes the 7:30 commuter train from Providence, transfers on the metro to the Park Avenue station, and walks to the Benson Controls building, where he works in the Electrical Engineering department. It is a tall, mirrored building, which stands across from another, taller, mirrored building, and the two faces reflect back onto each other infinite duplications of the same range of sky.

He lives and works in two different cities and, at moments, imagines getting lost somewhere in between. He goes through phases of driving to work, then taking the train, but the mode of transportation never changes the essential details of the fantasy: he disappears, en route.

Years ago, when he had been an employee at Benson for only five years, John decided that it was time for him to get to know some of his coworkers. He planted himself in front of the big printer and waited for a coworker to initiate conversation, just as an experiment. First ten minutes: a polite smile. Fifteen minutes: a suspicious look. Twenty-five: "Are you...?" (gesturing toward the printer), "No." Thirty-five: behind him, the water-cooler bubbled. Forty-five: a big peeled-back grin, and "Hi." "Hi." "How are you?" "Good, how are you?" "Good." "Good!" Her copies were ready, and she left. John stood there a couple more minutes figuring out whether that exchange actually counted for the purposes of his experiment, and his supervisor, Ray, came over with a concerned look on. "John, are you...all right? You okay?" Ray had a way of nodding as he asked a question, which through a kind of managerial hypnosis led to John nodding back.

John noticed soon after this that he was just as bad as the rest of them. Everyone in the office got important messages from John, tagged "priority." He would start them off with a clever opener and a chummy joke or two (nothing ribald or rude), and end with a request to be done ASAP(!). He "spoke to" young recruits about their computer-using habits and posted memos in the lounge about "someone" taking rolls of toilet paper from "the lav." But all of this was no one's fault. The fluorescence emanating from the low ceilings cast a uniform glow on every office, basking it all in anti-shadow— and no one saw the light at the end of their own tunnel vision.

Bad luck strikes in threes. First, the disaster in the boardroom; then, his computer crashing; and now, spilled coffee down the front of his shirt.

Rather than rush to clean it up, however, John sits in the glow of his computer illuminating the brown stain on the white shirt like a blacklight. Oddly, at the sight of the stain, John feels, not frustration, but a relief of sorts. Now that the shirt is ruined, he won't have to work so hard to keep it white. The computer failure (because Phil was unable to recover the data he lost) also broke over him like a breeze rather than a heavy wind, and left him oddly content.

John decides, impulsively, that his workday will finish early, and when he breaks for lunch, he will take the next train home. But, as John packs away his briefcase, the music slams into his head again.

It's a small world after all. It's a small world after all. It's a small world after all. It's a small, small world...It's a small world after all. It's a small world after all. It's a small world after all. It's a small, small world...

Wednesday, home alone in the afternoon, feels vaguely illicit. A minor crime, perhaps, like theft. But, like any crime, a whiff of idleness can whet the animal appetite; and John—a Pavlov's dog if there ever was one—finds himself salivating before the stimulus, yearning to be alone with nothing to do, on the train ride home.

As the train nears Providence, John entertains more ambitious criminal acts. He could quit his job, announce that he is leaving his home and family, and start a new life in a distant city. Or he could simply escape by walking through those doors, and leaping from that platform, onto the roadbed, to whatever destination. Somehow, the possibilities that build in him, with this contemplation—the options, choices, and potentialities—bring with them, not the expected rush of freedom, but the hollowness that comes from foreseeing too many futures, and living too few lives. John reaches into his briefcase, takes out an apple, and chews absently. The train soars along, making a sustained humming sound, nothing like the chugga-chugga-choo-choo of so many kids' books that, over the years, John has subjected his own children to.

John read, once, of a nineteenth-century German composer who, when riding the train for the first time, heard strains of music in the clicking of the wheels, and was inspired to write his first opera. John thinks of Phil's awful song, of all the awful music that floods the airwaves, and wonders whether his own tastes are compromised by the prevailing pop sensibility. He had been raised to listen to only the best music, but he had been privy to so many jingles and aimless melodies, and as a father had let his children glom on to any fashion. And now his son listens to Broadway musicals. He wonders now if he shouldn't have been the kind of father who pushes his children to excel in the world, to practice one thing—like music—until they understand nothing but music, the kind of brutal father whom the world judges harshly, but whom all secretly admire for forging a genius in the fire of his unappeasable discontent.

John wishes for anything, now, to replace the song that burrows, worm-like, into his foreskull. John looks down and focuses intently on the stain down the front of his shirt, hoping the power of vision will subdue his other senses. He chews the apple. He listens to the hum of the engine. He imagines himself as Lot's wife, a pillar of salt being blown away through an open window.

~

John flips on the tube and settles into his couch. Modern entertainment, it occurs to John, is about as dull as watching ash burn on a cigarette eternally. The most surprising thing about it—the reason, perhaps, that families throughout the world huddle around the TV like cavemen around the fire—is that the flicker never ends.

Idly, John wonders if exercise isn't the cure. It seems like only a year or two ago that the media was just beginning to tout the miracle of the natural high—the endorphin-releasing objects, such as the exercise bike, which now sat unused in the den. Having nothing else particularly to do, John dusts off the machine and sets it in front of the television, determined to master his despair in this way. He turns the volume up to maximum, and goes to the fridge to get a bottle of water.

John pedals faster when the commercials come on, as though his feet can accelerate time. Some white-toothed woman holds up her favorite pill—a formerly overweight mother with a box of Dieclan, say—and invites him to share in the pleasure. Then he grabs his water bottle and sucks off the cap, taking squirts like an excited baby rooting at the breast.

The mother in question is suspiciously beautiful, as though the effects of the pill offer not only relief from appetite, but cosmetic perfection, as well. In the final scene, she is wearing a spandex outfit, demonstrating her new, reformed figure for the viewing audience. By the time the next ad spot has begun, John finds his pedaling interrupted by a persistent erection. It grows to a painful hardness, constrained by the fabric of his shorts. Alone in the house, on a cloud-covered Wednesday afternoon, John guiltlessly pulls out his organ and strokes it, at first gently, then rapidly, as he continues to pedal on the machine.

After the commercials are over, and the beautiful women are gone, the daytime talk show starts again and John is left holding his pecker and staring at a panel of misfits. When he pulls at it now, the sensation is not arousal, but closer to the pressing of a button. And the song returns.

~

John sits on the piano bench and trills two keys, back and forth. He plays a few sharps, in the high range, where anything at all can sound like a harp. He doesn't know what it is. Perhaps he has seen too many live performances, heard too many records featuring piano virtuosos, seen too many movies where professional pianists who devote their life to the craft let their hands dance across the keys like limber insects. John feels, in this moment, as though to touch the piano would be to degrade the instrument, to bring it into the world of profane things—his world.

There is nothing especially wrong with his life, John reasons. There has been no recent tragedy, no trauma, no loss or unwanted gain. Ultimately, if things go on the way they have been going, John is promised another twenty years of healthy, productive life. His children will grow older, and become, like him, useful members of the world. They will have grandchildren, and add to the ranks of humanity. This meditation does not fail to fill him with the animal joy of inheritance, but it is the generality with which he can only conceive it, the unextraordinariness, which suffuses the world, the one he shares with all the other lonely souls, that seems to fold his life into a pile of neat, compact, and newly bleached clothes.

John touches the piano coyly, playing a few tentative notes in an almost-melody. He allows himself, passingly, to imagine creating something beautiful, original, and inspired. He closes his eyes and enters a reverie in which he is blessed with the skill of a master pianist, perfectly rendering the elusive, deep-dwelling song in him that obliterates other, more inferior, forms of music. When John returns from this reverie, he finds himself, instead, pounding frustratedly on the baby grand, the random *plunk, thwa, mroo, swash* of the hammers responding only to the angry bone of his hands, which seem to punch the keys, rather than play them.

128

John is walking. A light rain has begun. Heading south, on the east side of town, the streets of Providence taper into a single road, then dead-end at India Point, where a few old docks and bridges rise out of the water like the monuments of a dead civilization. The remnants of industry crowd the horizon, rusted and window-broken, shrouded by a perpetual halo of smog. Right now, a pair of students from Rhode Island School of Design are foraging nearby for the perfect assemblage of junk.

Historically disinclined toward self-pity, this sudden and inexplicable despair of the modern has taken John by surprise. After college, John had briefly studied Medicine, where he read that the ancient Greek physician, Hippocrates, believed in four bodily humors that governed the health and temper of men. Himself, he thought of as "bilious," prone to irrational anger; negative, perhaps; but not brooding in the weak-kneed, melancholic way of his son, Peter.

His wife, and his daughter, and his mother, too (now that he thinks of it), are joyful people, and he deeply and truly envies them their womanhood, which, not in every case, but certainly in their cases, imbue them with the capacity for love. The love they possess leaves its mark everywhere; the food they eat is full of it; the weave of their clothes, the lines of their faces, the pen lines they leave on their grocery lists.

In the argot of ancient Greece, the Gray family women are "sanguine."

"It means, 'full of blood'," said John to Abby, when she asked him, "what does it mean?"

Crouching near to the canal, watching the water flow effortlessly around the wharf—finding the bottommost point that gravity will allow—John tears. The profane world is filling up with too many worthless things, and John, brimming with this knowledge, feels the loose strands of himself give way.

He is too close to the edge. John fears that some deep impulse within him will leap into the river, and he is filled with fear of himself and his instincts. His breath comes fast, and the panic takes hold. Right now, as he fights for a lungful of air, he cannot imagine anything but this moment—a short span of self wavering like heat-lines from the street; not rising quite, but moving outward.

Yet there at his feet, below, like a buried root emerging from the dirt, an object floating in the water, the sight of which restores his calm: a small, smooth log in the shape of a boat, over-turned, bobbing up and down on a lump of algae, knocking against the pier. The clip-clop of wood against wood is a welcome song when the world, only a moment ago, threatened to go silent.

The sculpted boat is ugly and beautiful, and the sound it makes is rhythmic and arrhythmic, and the smell is low-tide.

It is a curious consolation that has come to balance the desolations of every other thing, but there it is, as clear a sign as though it had drifted out of the pages of a book.

Poetry Titles from Elixir Press

Fiction Titles

How Things Break by Kerala Goodkin
Nine Ten Again by Phil Condon
Memory Sickness by Phong Nguyen

Limited Edition Chapbooks

Juju by Judy Moffat
Grass by Sean Aden Lovelace
X-testaments by Karen Zealand
Rapture by Sarah Kennedy
Green Ink Wings by Sherre Myers
Orange Reminds You Of Listening
by Kristin Abraham
In What I Have Done & What I Have Failed To Do by
Joseph P. Wood
Hymn of Ash by George Looney
Bray by Paul Gibbons